McKensie Stewart

the Lost Letter

Tillman Publishing

Chapter 1

Marcia Rhodes waits quietly in Judge Jimmy McCaskill's chambers. Her Prada black suit jacket covers her soaked silk blouse. She fans her face for much-needed air.

The judge enters the chambers from a side door.

Marcia stands. "Your Honor."

Jimmy proceeds to unzip his robe and hang it in the closet without acknowledging Marcia's presence even though he summoned her to his office.

Marcia's eyes follow the judge's every move. Her fingertips fidget with the worn corners of her leather portfolio.

Jimmy plops down in his Italian leather chair. He rummages through his desk.

Marcia clears her throat just in case the judge forgot she was standing before him.

Jimmy cuts his eyes in Marcia's direction. "Please sit, Marcia."

Marcia makes a production of sliding up the sleeve of her jacket, flips her wrist around to glance at her watch.

"Marcia, am I keeping you from something?" Jimmy peers at Marcia over the rim of his glasses. He rests his back against the form-fitting chair, interlocking his hands on his midsection, his fingers barely touching.

"Actually, I do have another meeting in thirty minutes."

Jimmy slides the glasses up the bridge of his nose. "Oh, so let me get this right. My not starting our meeting on time is hindering you from something you have to do."

Marcia, regretting her last statement, decides not to respond. She avoids eye contact with him altogether.

Jimmy with a frown on his face starts his rant. "I feel the same way when you show up to my court late. Last week I threatened to fine you if you showed up late again." Jimmy snatches the glasses off his face and use them to point in Marcia's direction. "So here we are today; you show up fifteen minutes late."

"Judge, I can explain why I was late today."

Jimmy raises the hand that holds the glasses to stop Marcia from speaking. "I don't care why you were late. Last week was the last straw for me, but today you waltz in again late." He shakes his finger at Marcia. "You're testing me."

Marcia opens her purse and pulls out her checkbook. She leans forward for a pen off the judge's desk.

Jimmy snatches the pen holder from her reach. "I'm not going to let you off so easy to write the court a check. I had a conversation with Edward, the managing partner at your high-priced law firm. I hear you want to become partner."

Marcia leans in not to miss a single word from the judge.

"Do you think you deserve to make partner when you show up to my courtroom late?"

"My being late here and there shouldn't interfere with my making partner. I represent my clients with passion and enthusiasm, plus I have a high win rate. The people in the city come to me because they want a winner on their side."

Jimmy slaps the desk. "I'm glad you feel that way! I want you to represent Charlie Evans, pro bono with the same passion and enthusiasm you bring to the table as your paying clients."

"No! We have too many paying clients for my father to allow me to work pro bono." Marcia turns to the side and crosses her leg. *I just told the judge a thing or two.*

"Well, your father seems to differ. He says you have never done pro bono work, even in law school. His exact words were 'I think giving back to society will do her some good.'"

Marcia sucks up the air in the room with a deep breath.

Jimmy smiles wide as he hands Marcia the case file.

"Well, I guess we are done here," says Marcia while standing.

"Not exactly." Jimmy leans back in his chair and smooths his mustache with his index finger and thumb.

Marcia sits on the edge of the chair, staring blankly at the judge, not knowing what to expect next. "Yes, sir," says a deflated Marcia.

"I want this case to get as much attention as possible, so I scheduled an interview for you with Scotty Richards, on *Meeting of the Minds.*"

Marcia rolls her eyes. *Media coverage…great.* With all the sarcasm she can muster, she says, "Thank you, Your Honor."

"No worries, Marcia. I am always here to help. The appellate court reversed the lower court's decision, and your new client has a trial date in a few days. Tick tock." Jimmy chuckles and his belly moves up and down.

Marcia places the case file in her portfolio, stands, and walks toward the door.

"Marcia."

Marcia closes her eyes, her lips pursed. She slowly turns, her head tilted to the right with a forced smile. "Yes, Your Honor."

Jimmy's eyebrows furrow. "Don't ever disrespect me again in my court!"

"You have made it crystal clear all the reasons I need to be on time. It won't EVER happen again."

"I didn't think so."

Marcia turns and stomps out of Jimmy's office into the hall.

Marcia's phone rings, and her day brightens as she looks at the caller ID. "Hello."

"Where are you? I was in the area meeting a client and thought I would take the most beautiful woman out for a cup of coffee."

Marcia sighs heavily. "Hi Nick. I was summoned to Judge McCaskill's office. He is giving me grief about coming to court late."

Nick laughs. "You had to have known he wasn't going to let you disrespect him in his court for long."

"You sound like him."

"I still have time to meet you for an early lunch."

Marcia bites the outer corners of her lower lip, closes her eyes. "I would love to have lunch with you, but I have to go and see my new *pro bono* client."

"Oh snap! The judge gave you a pro bono case." Nick laughs again.

Marcia cannot help but smile at her boyfriend for poking fun at her.

"Okay, I'm sorry but the judge really got you where he wants you. You humiliated him and now it is his turn. Which case did he give you?"

Marcia unzips her portfolio and glances at the name on the folder. "Charlie Evans. Jimmy scheduled an interview for me, so I cannot meet you for lunch. I have to drive to Rikers."

"Oh, I remember this case. When I was a detective, I had Charlie for the murder of Sheryl Davis, but the rookie officer contaminated the crime scene. By the time I went back to try and salvage the case, I passed the bar and started practicing law."

"Do you still have a copy of the case file?"

"This is one of those cases that got away from me. From time to time, I pull the case file in hopes of finding new evidence."

Nick has a thought. "Why don't you come over for dinner to-night and I can share my notes with you."

"What about seven?"

"Seven it is."

Both Nick and Marcia end the call with a smile on their faces, remembering the last time they were together.

Chapter 2

*S*amantha Walker sits in front of the television. Warm tears stream down her cheeks; she uses the back of her hand to dry her face. The employees of Lehman Brothers, the fourth largest investment bank in the United States, exit the building with cardboard boxes; potted plants on one side, pictures of loved ones on the other. Samantha imagines what they could not fit in the box, they left behind. These people are not just employees; they are mothers, fathers, spouses, sisters, brothers who will go home and tell their loved ones they no longer have a job. When asked what happened, their only response will be "Greed."

She vividly remembers bursting into her manager Asher Wilson's office a year ago predicting the economic downfall.

Asher places his glasses on his desk, stands, and buttons the single button on his charcoal gray Brooks Brothers suit.

"Asher, do you have a minute?"

"I am headed out to lunch…what is it?"

Samantha shoves the stack of papers toward him. Asher takes two steps back, his briefcase in one hand, and throws up his free hand.

He knows what this outburst is about. Samantha barged in his office twice last year with a stack of papers raising concerns that the products they were offering would cause the economy to crash if their customers stopped paying their bills. She stands before him with the same concerned look on her face. "Sam, I don't have time for this today. I'm meeting a client for lunch and can't be late."

"My calculations are solid; this firm has further leveraged themselves with collateralized debt obligations. When the housing market collapses, so will the firm."

Asher walks to his glass door, opens it, and steps aside to allow Samantha to exit in front of him. She doesn't budge. "Sam, I have a client waiting for me."

"I feel like I have to save the company with what I know."

Asher releases the door handle and turns to Samantha. "You don't think I care about the firm? I'm managing partner and know this company will not be affected by whatever you have conjured in that pretty little head of yours."

Samantha ignores the misogynist comment. "I have the numbers to back my claims."

"Well, I have the numbers to back the six-figure bonus check I signed for you last month, which didn't bounce, nor did you return it to save the organization. So, if that's all I'll see you after lunch when we won't have this conversation again."

Asher opens the door once again, stands to the side to allow Samantha to walk in front of him; after all he is a gentleman.

"Have a nice lunch," she murmurs under her breath as she storms down the hall to her office and slams the door, the glass vibrating. She paces in front of her desk, then walks over to the window. Samantha looks down at the people below unknowing their world will crumble. The people who should alert them are turning their backs, even though it will cost the company its existence. Samantha shakes her head. She turns and walks to her desk, knowing what she has to do. She types her resignation letter, giving

Asher a two-week notice, knowing the company will not honor her request. She knows the company policy of resignations; she has too much access to confidential client information, plus the company does not want employees who are leaving to take clients with them to a new firm. She opens her briefcase and places her personal property, which consists of her engraved Mont Blanc pen and a photo of her and her mother, inside.

Samantha walks back to Asher's office and places the resignation letter on his desk. She takes the elevator downstairs to liquidate all her assets; actually, she purchased insurance and betted against the investment firms. If the housing market goes belly up, she will be rich, or richer. She knows she is being a hypocrite, but she knows she is right.

Samantha cries as she listens to the interviews, the former employees crying, the crawl at the bottom of the screen displaying the worthless stock of Lehman Brothers. She no longer can bear her heavy heart and sadness for her colleagues and friends, as she flips through the channels. Samantha stretches out on the sofa, her head on the throw pillow, her legs crossed at the ankle. She pauses on *Law & Order*; she has already seen this rerun many times over and she knows who the killer is. She turns the channel to her favorite station and host, Scotty Richards. Samantha yawns, lets out a quick sound of sleepiness. Even though she has not done anything physical, she is tired. She rests the remote on the coffee table.

Samantha's attention is back on Scotty's guest, Marcia Rhodes.

Marcia forces a smile, and her eyes squint while pumping her hands through clenched fists. She still cannot believe Judge McCaskill's gall making her take Charlie Evans' case pro bono.

———— ⊶⟨⟨⟩⟩⊷ ————

The producer counts Scotty down. "Marcia, thank you for joining me today. I do understand your busy schedule and that you cannot be here in person. Hopefully, the next interview you can be here with your client when he's fully exonerated."

Marcia nods. She takes a deep breath. In her head, reminds herself to be cool. "Scotty, thank you for having me on."

"When I heard you were taking the Charlie Evans case pro bono, I wanted to raise awareness of the case and the struggle the underprivilege experience when they can't afford legal counsel."

Marcia, not believing her own statement, says, "I do want to say people can get excellent counsel through public defenders. These men and women work hard to serve the public." Marcia is figuratively throwing up in her mouth.

"I think you're being modest; I'm looking at your record and you're definitely one of the best attorneys in the country."

Marcia pokes her chest out and genuinely smiles from ear to ear. Her conscience tells her to live up to her reputation. "Charlie Evans wrote Judge Jimmy McCaskill, professing his innocence." *If Jimmy is going to force me to take the case, I want him to be tied to whatever happens, good or bad. I read the case file and there isn't anything good about Charlie Evans.* She thinks back on the conversation she had with Nick earlier in the day about the unsolved murder of Sheryl Davis.

"I read the passion in his letters and knew I had to represent him. It is said, if you are Black, you are often jailed on who you are and not the merits of the case." says Marcia with as much white privilege as she can muster.

Samantha is drawn into the interview, bites her lower lip, and sits up.

"As you can see, I am standing outside of Rikers Island to let Charlie know I will represent him in his new trial."

"Is there new evidence in the case?" asks Scotty.

"In reviewing the case file, I found there is sufficient evidence of ineffective assistance of counsel, and the public defender was overloaded with other cases and missed key evidence. Charlie

Evans was a model citizen until police officers arrested him for no reason." Marcia blinks quickly—another white lie. "I have a court date next week for a new trial."

"I will have you back on after the judge rules in the case. I wish you and Mr. Evans good luck."

"Thank you but we don't need luck. We have the law on our side." Marcia marches into the prison to meet with her new client.

Chapter 3

*M*arcia glares at Charlie while he picks at the sardines in between his teeth with his long pinky nail. On the third try he finally wins his war with the smelly fish.

Marcia unfolds her arms and taps her acrylic index fingernail on the metal desk.

Charlie focuses his attention on his high society lawyer in front of him, folds his arms, and leans back in the chair. "Well, well, well, I saw you on television. You did pretty good. You had me believing your little performance."

"Tell me what happened the day you were arrested."

"When are you going to get me out of here? You know I'm innocent. You said so on television. Did you get a chance to meet that fine Scotty Richards in person? Is she married? Better yet, are you?" Charlie grins wide, his gold tooth shining in the light.

"Let's try this again. What happened the day you were arrested?"

Charlie licks his lips. "When I get out of prison, your house will be my first stop. I want to…"

Marcia leans across the table and points her finger in Charlie's face. "You listen here. I'm only here because I'm on Judge McCaskill's bad side, and my father agreed that I need to take your case. I have something to prove at my law firm, so you will do what I say."

Charlie folds his hands in front of him and casually leans face-to-face with Marcia. "What are you trying to prove? Are you trying to make a name for yourself? Are you going to use little ole me to build your career? Now, that's steep." Charlie crosses his arms. "If I help you, there is something I need from you. You know how it goes, something for something."

"I'm not going to dignify your inappropriate comment with a response. I don't make deals with convicts."

Charlie smirks. "Okay, Miss Rhodes, you are right. I am a convict, but you need me just as much as I need you." The slick smile on his face makes Marcia for a second regret taking the case. She sighs. She does not have any other choice. Marcia interlocks her fingers, her right thumb crossing the left. She rubs them together to calm her nerves. "Look, I have a job to do and that's getting you out of here."

Charlie rubs his hands together. "So, we are back to my original question. When are you getting me out of here?"

"Charlie, it doesn't work that way. We do have a new trial date where I will present new evidence to demonstrate your innocence that was not presented in your previous trial. I came here in part to let you know I'm your new attorney and to look you in your eyes to find out if you did it or not."

"Well," says Charlie.

"Well, what?"

"Am I worthy for you to take my case?"

"Stop playing games. I'm going to ask you only once. Did you kill Janie?"

Charlie chews on the side of his cheek. "No, I didn't kill her. I was framed by the police."

Marcia was not interested in his last comment. How many times has she heard that statement? She could buy a second home in the Hamptons. Marcia's eyes search Charlie's soul. *Just look at him. Who the hell does he think he is? He may be the King of Con, but I can sniff bullshit a mile away.* "Well then, it looks like you have yourself a lawyer." It's not like Marcia has any choice on whether she takes the case or not; she is indebted to the judge.

Chapter 4

*B*ruce, the corrections officer, listens intently to Andrew, the officer on the other end of the radio. Bruce shakes his head. "I'm escorting Charlie back to his cell now. Charlie, I need you to move to the right."

Charlie, shackled, shuffles to the right. "What's going on?" Just as he asks the question, a gurney with a white sheet covering a body exits his cell. His mouth flaps open. "Bruce, is that Charles?"

"Yeah, Charles passed away while you were with your lawyer."

"Can I say goodbye to him?"

Bruce takes his work cap off, scratches his bald head, and places the cap back on. "Yeah, I don't see any harm in your saying goodbye."

Bruce nods toward Andrew, who stops. "Charlie wants to say a few words to his cellmate."

Charlie shuffles toward the body, and Andrew pulls back the white sheet covering the deceased body of Charlie's friend and cellmate Charles Walker. Charlie fights back tears and swallows hard to clear the lump in his throat. "Can I go to my cell now?"

Charlie's head is low to shield the stares of the onlooking inmates. Bruce leads him down the cellblock to his cell.

Bruce unlocks the cuffs and shackles. "Are you okay? I know it's a lot to take in, Charles dying."

"Man, I'm okay." Charlie sniffles.

Bruce, still not convinced Charlie is okay, lingers in the cell a little while longer. "I'll tell you what. I will try to hold off anyone giving you a cellmate for a few days so you can get yourself together." Bruce places his hand on Charlie's shoulder.

"Thank you, man." Charlie knows Bruce is going out of his way to be nice, and he genuinely appreciates the gesture. "I just need to get my thoughts together. Charles was here one day and gone the next. I was in the room with my lawyer for less than an hour. Gone just like that." He snaps his fingers.

Charlie shakes his head. A tear falls on his orange jumpsuit and transforms to a small wet spot. Bruce takes that as a sign to give Charlie some space. The cell door clinks shut behind Bruce.

Charlie gazes at the floor. If his father were alive when he was growing up, maybe he would have taken a different path. The last time Charlie saw his father was on the Fourth of July.

(Twenty years earlier…)

Sharon, Charlie's mother, enjoys the holidays. It is an excuse to invite friends and family over. No one needs a call from Sharon; they all cook and bake their specialties and tell Sharon what they will bring.

Sharon beams with joy seeing everyone turn out. She goes from cluster to cluster, catching up on what she missed from the last Fourth of July. Sharon, always a hospitable host, puts the needs of others before hers, but today is different. She scans the guests; they are either deep in conversation or feeding their faces with LP's famous potato salad or licking their fingers on Mickey's fall-off-the-bone ribs. Mickey is a Southerner true, and true he only uses his home-made mustard-based barbeque sauce. If you ask him for ketchup-based barbeque sauce, he beckons anyone around and tells them you asked for the disgraced sauce. They tease you the entire day, calling you "the sellout." Sharon hears Mickey teasing Enes about the sauce, but Enes received the lashing last year, so he is just messing with Mickey.

Suddenly, Sharon stops, not sure if she is sweating like a pig from the oppressive heat of climate change or a hot flash. She lifts the braids off her back and wipes her neck with a damp hand towel. Then she twists the braids and makes a knot to keep the synthetic hair off her back to allow her floral short-sleeve dress to dry.

Sharon snatches the last bottled water out of the cooler, and within three gulps the entire bottle is gone. She disposes of the evidence in the nearby recycle bin and wipes her mouth with the back of her hand. Still thirsty, Sharon walks in the house anticipating the chill of the air conditioner on her skin. Goose bumps form on Sharon's arms, and she turns to the left to enter the kitchen through the swinging doors that separate the kitchen from the living room. Sharon's eyes widen. "What the hell is going on?" she screams.

"Sharon, I can explain," Daniel stammers in a pleading wail as he pulls up his boxers and khaki cargo shorts. Dorothy adjusts her underwear and smooths her dress in the front and in the back.

Sharon speaks directly to Daniel, her stare deadly. "You can explain, explain what? Let me hear this miraculous story." Sharon has Daniel in her crosshairs and Dorothy in her peripheral vison. Dorothy slowly moves. "Where do you think you are going?" barks Sharon.

"I don't want to interrupt. I should be going."

Sharon snatches the knife from the butcher block. Dorothy slowly steps backward, putting distance between her and Sharon, the imprint of the knife on the palm of her hand.

"Baby, look at me, put the knife down. Nobody wants any trouble," says Daniel. The last time she caught him cheating, Sharon ran the girl out of the house and fussed all day.

That day, Sharon had showered and made a place on the sofa to sleep for the night. She drifted off to sleep only to dream about the one thing she was trying to escape, her husband having sex with another woman in the bed they shared together as husband and wife. She sat up, put her slippers on, and rambled through the garage. She walked up the stairs to the bedroom and doused the flammable, clear liquid on the bed and her husband. Just as Sharon struck the match, Daniel felt the cold liquid on his body and smelled the fumes. He jumped from the bed and tackled his wife. In the tussle the match went out.

Now, Sharon waves the knife in the air in her quest for answers. "You are right, nobody wants any trouble, but you caused it." Hot tears flow down her cheeks. "Dorothy, you are my best friend. Why did you do this to me? How long has this been going on?" The room is quiet enough to hear a church mouse. "The two of you owe me an explanation, so someone better start talking."

The two speak simultaneously. "One at a time...I need to hear this." Sharon uses the knife to point in Dorothy's direction.

Dorothy pipes up, "It just happened today, honestly."

"She started flirting with me and one thing led to another."

Sharon's eyes narrow on Dorothy. She shifts her weight from one leg to another.

Dorothy takes several small steps backward. She quickly decides to save herself and turns on Daniel, blaming him for their indiscretion. "You told me at last month's book club you wanted me."

Daniel murmurs under his breath, "You haven't read a book a day in your life."

Dorothy points her finger in Daniel's face. "Are you kidding me now? You are going to throw shade on me after I let you get a piece!"

"Me and everyone in town had several pieces, like a sweet potato pie during Thanksgiving."

The back-and-forth between the man she adores and her best friend causes Sharon's head to throb. She closes her eyes to stop the room from spinning. Her grip on the knife tightens and she uses the back of her hand to wipe the tears from her eyes, leaving behind black mascara streaks. Her breathing intensifies, her eyes pop open, and her head shifts from side to side. Who will I stab first? Daniel, her husband of twenty years, two miscarriages and countless mistresses. She gave her life to this man, vowing never to leave him in front of friends, family, and most importantly God.

Dorothy, a friend since high school, borrowed thousands of dollars throughout the years and never attempted to pay the money back. In high school Dorothy debunked the rumors that she slept with Sharon's boyfriend, Michael. Sharon took Dorothy's side because friendship has always been sacred to her. Perhaps Michael could have been her way out; she could have had a different life. Michael is an attorney living in South Carolina with two children, married. Dorothy robbed her of the life she could have had. She is the target—she is to blame for the current situation.

Charlie, standing behind the swinging door, hears the entire conversation. He barges into the kitchen, and the swinging door knocks his mother on the floor; the knife flies out of Sharon's hand just inches from Dorothy's feet. All eyes on Dorothy, she scrambles to the floor to secure the knife, her only ticket out of the house.

In the commotion, Charlie's fight-or-flight instinct is to protect his mother. He grabs another knife from the butcher's block and charges toward Dorothy, stabbing her in the stomach. Dorothy falls to the floor, lying in a puddle of her own blood. Charlie stabs Dorothy over and over, in and out of the tough flesh, hitting bone each time. Blood splatters the floor and cabinets.

Daniel tackles Charlie and pries the knife out of his hand. Charlie falls backward. "Oh, no, son! What have you done?"

Charlie bites the right corner of his bottom lip. His eyes lower to the floor. "She was going to destroy our family. I had no choice. I saw the two of you together, and you were both laughing behind Mama's back. You said you liked the way she touched you."

Sharon sprints to the front door, locks it, and bursts into the room screaming, "Stop talking! What are we going to do with the body? We have twenty guests outside."

Daniel now back on his wife's team says, "Let's take her body to the basement until everyone leaves. It will give us time to figure out what to do."

Sharon thinks about the suggestion. "What are we going to tell her husband?" The three of them look at each other with blank stares.

Chapter 5

*D*aniel searches the cabinet under the sink for the large lawn and garden trash bags; the regular bags will not do. He uses the kitchen shears to cut along the seams of several bags. Daniel lays the plastic bags next to Dorothy's body. "Charlie, give me a hand. Grab her legs and I will grab her arms; place the body on the trash bags." Daniel and Charlie work in silence, and the two wrap the bags around Dorothy's body. Daniel secures their haphazard work with electrical tape. Slowly they drag the body toward the door to the basement.

Sharon on her own mission searches under the kitchen sink cabinet for cleaning supplies to remove the crimson bloodstain from the floor. She dips the head of the mop in the bleach and water mixture. She mops the entire floor twice, wringing the mop dry. Sharon pours the soiled water down the sink in the kitchen. Then turns to the task of wiping down the cabinets.

Bam. Bam. Bam. Sharon jumps at the pounding at the front door. She dries her hands on her dress and walks toward the door. Slowly she opens the door and is face-to-face with her neighbor

Mabel. "Girl, what are you doing with the door locked with a yard full of people. I have to go to the little girl's room." Mabel barges in and heads in the direction of the downstairs bathroom.

Sharon rushes past Mabel to block her entrance to the bathroom. "Mabel, the downstairs bathroom is broken. You will have to use the one upstairs."

Mabel lifts a single eyebrow. "The toilet was working fine earlier."

Sharon rubs her right arm. "You know with so many people the bathroom is likely to stop working. You know…"

Mabel turns and shakes her head on her journey to the upstairs bathroom and huffs under her breath, "The bathroom was working earlier. Your husband's a plumber. He cannot fix the bathroom. I have to walk up all these stairs. You know I have a weak bladder. These women want to say they are married with these no-good men."

Sharon stands at the bottom of the stairs, arms folded, straining to hear the bathroom door close. Once the coast is clear Sharon dashes into the kitchen.

In the meantime, Daniel and Charlie are three steps into their journey down the basement steps, Daniel carrying the bulk of the weight on him walking backward. "Turn on the light; it's hard for me to find the steps the further we go into the basement."

Charlie attempts to pull the dangling string to turn on the light but misses, shoving the body into Daniel. Daniel loses his balance and rocks back and forth, grabbing the rail to steady himself. "That was a close call. I almost fell backwards." They both chuckle.

Charlie takes a second attempt at the string; the light illuminates the basement.

Sharon appears out of nowhere. "Hey, you guys need to hurry up. I am going…."

Charlie, startled at the sound of his mother's voice, shoves the body into his father and lets go of Dorothy's feet. Daniel loses his balance and lands headfirst on the concrete floor of the unfinished basement. Dorothy's body bounces down the remaining nine stairs, landing next to Daniel. Sharon rushes past Charlie to her husband lying on the floor. Blood slowly trickles from the corners of Daniel's mouth. Sharon lays her head on her husband's chest and softly cries.

Mabel grumbles as she makes her way downstairs. She stops at the sound of a loud thump coming from the direction of the kitchen. Carefully, Mabel opens the swinging doors with both hands. She creeps into the kitchen, scans the room, and walks toward the open basement door, where she hears crying. Mabel appears at the top of the stairs when she hears Charlie ask his mother, "Ma, is Daddy dead?"

Mabel's eyes divert to the bottom of the stairs to Sharon with her head on Daniel's chest and what looks like a body wrapped in a trash bag. Before Sharon can respond to her son, Mabel exits the house to join the other guests outside.

"Ma, what are we going to do?"

"Charlie, give me a minute to think."

Charlie sits at the top of the stairs until his mother gives him further instructions.

Sharon takes her husband's pulse.

Charlie whispers, "Is he dead?"

"Yes, son, your daddy is dead."

"What are we going to do?"

"I don't know."

"You better think of something; someone is knocking on the door."

Chapter 6

Once outside, Mabel's eyes shift from person to person doing a mental headcount. The only two people missing are Daniel and Dorothy. Mabel decides to sit perched next to Justin, Dorothy's husband. She believes that Dorothy is in the trash bag.

Sharon and Charlie are runners for anyone who wants anything in the house, even escorting people in the house to use the bathroom.

Sharon, mentally and physically exhausted from the heat, repeated trips to the house, and the betrayal and the death that surrounds her, has had enough. Around six o'clock, she tells everyone she needs to get up early and needs everyone to leave.

The crowd slowly disperses, and Justin wanders around the yard looking for his wife.

Mabel blocks Sharon's path to the trash can. "What are you hiding?"

"I don't know what you mean."

"What was going on with escorting people to the bathroom?"

"Like I said, the bathroom downstairs was broken."

"Excuse me, Sharon. Have you seen Dorothy? I was having so much fun catching up with classmates and neighbors, I forgot the last time I saw her."

"Oh, Justin, Dorothy said she wasn't feeling well and left the cookout about thirty minutes ago."

"Why didn't she tell me? I would have walked her home."

"Yeah, she said she wanted you to enjoy yourself and not fuss over her."

Justin smiles. His wife is thoughtful. "Do you need help cleaning up?"

"Oh, no!" Sharon exclaims. "Charlie is around here someplace; he can help me clean up."

"I won't take no for an answer." Justin starts throwing empty plates and cups in the trash.

Sharon has forgotten Mabel is still standing next to her until she chimes in, "What happens when Justin goes home, and his wife isn't there? How long do you think it will take for him to call the police? The first place they will look is the last place she was seen, which is here. What are you going to do?"

Through clenched teeth Sharon responds, "I am so tired of everyone asking me what to do." She starts crying.

"Pull yourself together and stop that crying. You have a son you need to think about."

Sharon uses her fingertips to dry her tears.

In a low whisper, Mabel asks what happened to Dorothy and Daniel. Sharon tells her everything. Mabel, never at a loss for words, is speechless. It's a good thing because Justin is headed in their direction.

"Sharon, I think everything is cleaned up out here. I will be going now unless you need something else."

Sharon pauses, perspiration drips down her back, and her heart races. Mabel puts her hand on Sharon's shoulder, leans toward her, and whispers in her ear, "I know you will do the right thing."

Mabel directs this part of the conversation so Justin can hear. "Well, I don't want to overstay my welcome, so I better get going." Mabel gives Sharon and Justin a weak smile and walks to her home next door.

Sharon replays the conversation between her and nosy Mabel. What happens when Justin goes home, and Dorothy isn't there?

"Sharon, are you okay? You don't look well. Sit down."

"Justin, I need to tell you something and I don't know where to start."

"This sounds serious. What's this all about?"

Sharon sits down and invites Justin to have a seat next to her. She explains finding Dorothy and her husband in a compromising position in the kitchen. She waits, ready to hear Justin yell at her for lying or better yet call the police. Justin falls back in his chair and pounds his fists on his thigh. "She said she would never cheat again."

"What?"

"This wasn't Dorothy's first-time cheating. Six months ago, Dorothy was pregnant."

"That's a good thing, right?"

"I can't have kids; I'm sterile."

Sharon's hands cover her mouth.

"I will deal with Dorothy when I get home." Justin's face is long enough to drag the ground. He stands to leave.

"What do you mean deal with Dorothy?"

"I am going to ask her for a divorce. I cannot deal with the lies and cheating. I am so mad; I could kill her."

Sharon asks Justin to sit down again. She has more to share. She tells him about the death of his wife and what happened. Justin is unfazed that his cheating wife is dead. Sharon stands and leads Justin into the house and then to the basement, where the two bodies lie at the bottom of the stairs. Justin takes the steps two at a time until he is kneeling next to the body in the black trash bag. Justin uses his fingers to pierce the bag, and once he has an opening, he uses both hands to pull the bag entirely open. He closes his dead wife's eyes. Sharon stands at the top of the stairs with her arms around Charlie, looking down on Justin. Justin stands. "What now?"

"We need to get rid of the bodies."

Justin scratches his head and pauses for a moment. "I have the perfect spot. Charlie, do you think you can help me get these bodies up the stairs?"

"Yeah, sure."

"I can help, too," Sharon chimes in.

Justin reaches in his back pocket and gives his keys to Sharon. "I want you to go to my house, get the blue tarp out of the garage, and drive my Ford Explorer back so I can haul the bodies away."

Eagerly, Sharon agrees. She needed someone else to tell her what to do. She jogs down the street to Justin's home and finds what she is looking for; she closes the garage and drives back down the street to her home. Sharon opens the trunk and spreads the tarp to cover the entire length and width of the trunk.

⸺ ⸻ ((◉)) ⸻ ⸺

Mabel enjoys her warm bath, washing off the perspiration from earlier in the day. She dries off and slathers her body in lotion, standing in the center of her bedroom. Her phone rings. "Hello."

"Hey, Mabel. How was the cookout?" asks Josephine.

"It was good. I was able to catch up with so many people I haven't seen since the last cookout."

"How are you doing? I know this was a hard day for you and Michaela paying respect to Larry."

"Michaela will always be a daddy's girl. She will be fine. I will shower her with love."

Mabel stops at the slight movement of the shadows moving

in the yard below in Sharon's yard. Justin, Sharon, and Charlie carry two long objects wrapped in a black bag to the back of Justin's SUV. Is that Justin's truck? Mabel walks back to her bathroom, takes her robe off the hook on the back of the door, and puts it on. She snuggles into the robe and turns off the lamp in her bedroom for a better view. "Josephine, let me give you a call tomorrow."

"Good night."

Those have to be the bodies of Dorothy and Daniel. She was right. Sharon did tell Justin what happened to Dorothy.

Mabel continues to watch as Justin drives out of Sharon's driveway and down the street past his house and out of the community.

Sharon and Charlie go back into the house. Sharon pours herself a large glass of wine. One, two, three gulps, and the wineglass is empty. Sharon's hands start to steady, her nerves calm.

Charlie walks behind his mother. "Where is Justin taking Daddy and Dorothy?"

"He's taking them to the apartment building on the corner of Caldwell and Stonewall."

Charlie takes in the information his mother tells him. "Ma, I walk uptown a couple of times a week—there isn't a building on that corner."

"Son, there isn't a building yet. They are going to pour the foundation in the morning." Sharon gives her son a weak smile.

Sharon has finished the bottle of wine when Justin rings the doorbell. Justin and Sharon chat for several minutes. He assures her that he handled disposing of the bodies. Sharon closes the door behind Justin and turns to Charlie, who has never left her side.

"Ma, are you okay?"

"Yes, just a little tipsy. Charlie, you have to promise me that you will never bring up this situation to anyone. I mean anyone ever again."

"If someone asks where's Daddy, what do I say?"

"I don't know. He ran off with another woman; that's the story I will tell."

"I don't know if I can say that."

"If you repeat a lie long enough, even you will believe it."

Charlie wrinkles his brow, digesting what his mother just said.

"Go ahead and get some sleep. I love you."

"I love you, too."

"Don't forget; we will never speak of this night ever. Promise."

Charlie walks over to his mother to pinky swear on their secret. "Promise."

Sharon kisses him on the forehead, and he walks up the stairs to his bedroom. He is too tired to take a shower. So, he peels off his clothes, puts on his PJ's, and gets into bed. As soon as his head hits the pillow, he falls into a deep slumber.

Sharon starts on a second bottle of wine, trying to forget two people died in her home, one of whom was her husband, who she adored even if he was a lying cheat. Sharon drinks enough wine that she passes out on the sofa.

Chapter 7

Two years later, Sharon is dark and withdrawn, only moving through the motions of living. She cooks, cleans the house, and goes to work to support her and Charlie. Even though church was a part of her routine, she can't bring her lie to the doors of the church. She has stopped going to church because she believes God isn't pleased with the cover-up. Church was the glue that held her family together. Sharon told Charlie to lie, but the secret is eating her up inside. She disappointed her Heavenly Father, and today she needs to make it right.

Charlie bounces down the stairs to the kitchen to find his mother standing over a pot of grits and humming "Amazing Grace." Charlie takes a seat at the table, tucking the paper napkin in his t-shirt at the neck. Charlie's eyes follow his mother from the stove to the refrigerator to the table. Charlie wants his mother to be well, but her cheerfulness is odd. Strange…he hasn't seen her this happy since before the incident that he isn't supposed to talk about.

"Ma, is everything all right?"

"Why do you ask, baby?"

"You seem different today, happier."

"Baby, today is a wonderful day, and I am going to make peace with what happened to Dorothy and Daniel."

"I thought you told me never to talk about it." Charlie gives his mother a puzzled look.

"This will be the last time we will discuss it. Eat your breakfast and I'm going to head off to work. The bus will be at the stop in five minutes. I need to hurry." She kisses Charlie on the forehead and wishes him well. His mother closes the door behind her and walks down the street toward the bus stop.

Charlie, a protective son, always watches his mother from the time she leaves the house to the bus stop. Today is no different—the first watch begins in the kitchen until she crosses the street and turns left to walk on the sidewalk. Charlie runs to the living room for a different view. After the death of his father, he has been the man of the house, and he vowed to his mother that he would look out for her. Charlie discerns from his mother's steps they aren't rushed. Sharon stops one house short of the bus stop; if she continues to drag her feet, she will miss the bus. Charlie quickly exits the house to investigate his mother's troubling behavior.

Mr. Earl, the bus driver, slows the bus to make the right turn onto Charlie's street. Mr. Earl picks up speed after clearing the corner. Sharon slowly starts to walk again, but instead of moving toward the bus stop, she darts in the path of the bus onto the street.

Mr. Earl slams on the brakes, but it is too late. Sharon's body is dragged until the bus stops.

"Ma, no!" shouts Charlie. He races to the bus.

The driver swings open the door and runs down the steps professing his innocence. "She jumped into the street. I tried to stop but it was too late."

The passengers exit the bus and surround Sharon's lifeless body.

Mabel, enjoying her morning coffee on the porch, drops her coffee mug. Coffee splatters everywhere. She scampers to the kitchen and places a call to 911.

Ms. Josephine, a widower who lives on the other side of Mabel and a friend of both Sharon and Mabel, takes Charlie in to live with her and her daughter Michaela. Mabel stops short of telling Josephine what she knows about Charlie but warns her she needs to be careful bringing someone who witnessed so much devastation in his life into her home. Josephine just thought she meant his mother's death. She soon learns Charlie is a troubled boy.

He first becomes mischievous by committing petty crimes. He steals candy and gum from the neighborhood store. He doesn't need to steal. Ms. Josephine is a retired superintendent of the local school district and has the insurance money from her deceased husband, Larry, to live off. She takes good care of Charlie and even tries to get him counseling. Charlie walks out of his first session and vows he will never return. He stays with Ms. Josephine until he turns seventeen and drops out of school only to live from one girlfriend's house to another. His petty crimes turn serious when he starts snatching purses in the local park. One night, he is hanging out on the local corner with his homeboys, when this girl, who looks twenty-five, struts in front of them. The age doesn't matter; he wants to take a peek inside her Gucci purse. His eyes bounce from her purse to her ass.

"Hey, sexy mama," shouts Charlie as he grabs his crotch and follows the girl.

The young girl flaps her hand in the air to acknowledge the rude guy catcalling but refuses to stop; in fact, she picks up the pace.

"Sexy mama, slow down. I got something to tell you."

The unsolicited name calling makes her feel uncomfortable; she tugs on her mid-thigh tartan plaid pleated skirt trying to make it longer. She glances over her shoulder to gauge how far behind her he is. Charlie balls his fist and punches her in the face. She stumbles backward into the alley and falls on the ground, scraping her knees and tearing her knee-length socks. The girl nurses her left cheek with her hand.

"Well, well, Miss High Society Girl, what are you doing on this side of town slumming it with us lowlifes?"

The girl sniffles and stands, and blood trickles down her knees.

Charlie wags his finger at her. "You have a Black boyfriend? You know your kind like the brown-skinned fellows."

"I don't want any trouble. Take my purse." She extends the purse to him.

Charlie takes his time circling her; with each step the girl feels more and more threatened. She walks in tiny circles, not taking her eyes off him. Offering the purse didn't work, so she tries another angle. "Take my wallet." The girl reaches in her purse, but instead of retrieving her wallet, she pulls out pepper spray and squirts in the direction of her violator.

Charlie, quick on his feet, moves out of the direct path of the cayenne pepper's spray. "I wish you wouldn't have done that."

Charlie's hands wrap around the girl's neck, and he squeezes so hard she gasps for air, but Charlie's grip tightens. The girl eyes roll in the back of her head; he holds his grip a little longer to ensure his victim is dead. Charlie scavenges through the purse and into the wallet—no money, just weed. She must have just made a purchase. He looks at the driver's license. Sheryl Davis was twenty-one years old. He snatches her necklace and coughs up clumps of mucus and spits on Sheryl. He places the license and weed in his back pocket. Charlie decides not to share his newfound treasure with his homeboys but to keep the weed all to himself.

Chapter 8

Charlie strolls in the house he is shacking up in with his girlfriend, Elizabeth. Elizabeth is lying on the sofa with one hand on her forehead, the other with a washcloth over her mouth. "Hey, baby, you want to take a hit?" He shakes the weed baggie. Charlie licks his lips, anticipating the euphoric sensation of the weed going through his body.

Elizabeth does not hold back. "Charlie, I'm pregnant."

"What do you mean you're pregnant?"

"Don't act like you don't know how it works!"

"I know how it works. I'm surprised that's all. I'm excited." Charlie rushes to Elizabeth's side and rubs her belly. "I know that look in your eyes…you're stressed. I will take care of you and the baby."

Elizabeth sits up. "You know my father will force us to get married."

"I'm down for that. Let us get married tomorrow, then tell your parents."

Elizabeth stands and paces the floor, thinking of what she will wear to the courthouse. Elizabeth frowns. "Charlie, we can get married, but you need to get a job. How can you support us if you are not working? You cannot keep stealing your way through life. We are going to have a family."

"After we get married, I will find a job, but first I will smoke this weed." Charlie rolls the joint to smoke. Meanwhile, Elizabeth runs around the house finding something to wear for her big day.

Chapter 9

Charlie upheld his end of the bargain, and he and Elizabeth married. Charlie found a job and they brought into the world a healthy baby boy, Samuel, named after Elizabeth's grandfather. Charlie held onto the job as a cook for five years until he and his new supervisor got into a confrontation. Fred was correcting Charlie on how to be more efficient while prepping the meals for the day. Charlie, one who did not like to be told he was wrong, told Fred a thing or two about his poor leadership. This was not the first time Charlie mouthed off to him, but the circumstance was different this time. Charlie told Fred he was wrong in front of his employees. Fred made a snap decision to fire Charlie to maintain his dignity and respect of his subordinates.

Charlie promised himself he would get another job before Elizabeth knew he was fired. In the meantime, he needed to keep up the pretense he was still working. So, every day Charlie would get dressed and leave the house like he was going to work. He spent his days hanging out on the corner until it was time to go home for the evening.

━━━━━━⟫⟪◉⟫⟪━━━━━━

On this particular day, a beautiful lady walks in front of him and into the coffee shop. Charlie, not one to drink coffee, but who does love to meet a beautiful woman, walks in and takes a seat beside her on the single chairs along the window facing the street, and the two introduce themselves. Janie Matthews extends her hand to Charlie. The two talk for an hour, laughing and creating a true bond. Janie takes a deep breath, and she gets bold. "Would you like to come back to my house for something stronger?" Janie stands and puts her purse under her arm.

"Sure." Charlie licks his lips. His eyes follow her every move.

The two leave the coffee shop and walk to her apartment hand in hand. They make love on the sofa and move to the bedroom. The two spend all afternoon together. Charlie calls Elizabeth to tell her he is working a double shift. Elizabeth does not question Charlie's motives; they can use all the money they can get. She tells him to be safe walking home from work.

Charlie continues to make love to Janie. She orders Chinese food, and they eat in bed, talking about their dreams. Janie expresses her need to escape and move someplace far way; she doesn't care where but is leaving tomorrow. Charlie is bogged down in his responsibilities of life, the child, wife, and now unemployment. He too wants to leave the city behind; why not start over with someone as intriguing as Janie? He takes a deep breath and the two plan to leave the next day at the same time they met earlier in the day, but they will meet at her apartment. Charlie thinks she is running from something, but he is too. Charlie makes a mental list of all the items he will carry with him on his new adventure with Janie. He can't pack just yet; he doesn't want to alarm Elizabeth. The two part ways. Charlie kisses his new love interest and skips down the hall and exits the building. Unbeknownst to him he lets Janie's estranged husband, Edwin, into the building. Edwin, who has been taking pictures of them all afternoon, recognizes Charlie as the guy who stole his wife from him.

Edwin takes the stairs to Janie's apartment and knocks on the door. Janie opens the door without looking through the peephole, thinking Charlie left something behind, and is face-to-face with her abusive husband. "Who were you with this afternoon?" Edwin demands while pushing his wife and closing the door behind him.

"Nobody."

"Don't lie to me. I followed you all afternoon."

"He's just a friend."

"I'm not good enough for you? You have to meet a stranger in a coffee bar."

Janie tightens her grip on the collar of her robe. Edwin leans to the left and slaps her with the back of his hand with all the force of his 230 pounds. Janie flies across the room onto the floor. She crawls backward, trying to get away from him but going nowhere at all. Edwin walks toward Janie and steps on her right hand, breaking the bones. "Where do you think you are going?"

He leans his weight on her hand. "Stop, please stop," begs Janie.

"Did you tell him to stop this afternoon when you were having sex with a man not your husband?"

"Edwin, I promise I will never do anything like this again."

"You're right. You won't." Edwin takes a knife out of his holster.

"Please stop. I'm sorry," she repeats over and over.

After he tortures her mentally, Edwin deals the last blow to her heart with the stab of the knife. Janie gives up the fight she has been fighting for ten years. Edwin would never sign the divorce papers. He quit his job to dodge the law on stalking his wife to make her life a living hell. He found a way to do this every waking hour of the day.

Edwin waits in the apartment in the wee hours of the morning and leaves through the back exit of the stairs. He disappears into the night, satisfied. If he can't be with his wife, no one will.

Chapter 10

The next morning, Elizabeth rushes to the car to get Sam to daycare so she can get to the breadwinning job of the family. She kisses Charlie on the lips. "Have a good day."

"You, too." Charlie stares at his feet.

Elizabeth rounds the corner to start her day. Charlie quickly packs his bag, remembering everything he thought about the night before to place in his duffle bag. In reality, he wants to carry more than he originally thought, so he adds the only suit he owns to the mix. He shoves clothing and video games into his bags. At the point of no more room, Charlie is forced to zip the bag.

Charlie hurries to Janie's apartment and follows a delivery man into the building. He takes the elevator to Janie's floor. The door ajar, Charlie is excited she anticipated his visit. "Good morning, my love. How are you? Oh shit!" Charlie drops his bag and races over to Janie's body.

Edwin, waiting for Janie's lover to appear, calls the police. Within minutes, the police are on the scene due to the police satellite station two blocks over. Charlie hears the sirens and walks to the bedroom for a second glance of any of his personal belongings from the night before. All is clear. However, he stops in his tracks when he sees Janie's purse. He rambles through her purse and finds her wallet. He throws the wallet in his bag and rushes to the door. It is too late. Amanda Block and her partner Adam Warner, standing on the other side of the door with their guns drawn, stop Charlie. He drops his bag and walks backward with his hands in the air.

Amanda moves her head to peer over Charlie's left shoulder and sees a lifeless body. She calls for backup and an ambulance.

"What's your name?"

"Charlie Evans."

"How do you know the victim?"

"We just met yesterday."

Amanda's eyes narrow to the duffle bag and suitcase on the floor. "Are you taking a trip?"

"Yeah, Janie and I were going away together."

Adam walks into the bedroom. "There's not any luggage in the bedroom."

Amanda's gun is pointed at Charlie as she takes Janie's pulse. "She's dead. What happened?"

"When I left last night, she was happy, and we planned to run away together."

"Run away from what?"

"Life."

The crime scene investigation unit swarms the apartment dusting for fingerprints and evidence.

"Is this your bag?" asks Adam.

Charlie nods his head up and down.

Adam bends down and unzips the bag and pulls out Janie's wallet.

"Before you accuse me of anything, I did steal Janie's wallet, but it was after I found her dead. I thought she didn't have any use for it, so I took it."

Adam and Amanda give each other side glances. Amanda reads him his Miranda Rights while cuffing him. She leads him out of the apartment building into the back of the police car.

Edwin, standing across the street, watches Janie's lover escorted out of the building and into the back of the police car. He has won. He turns and disappears into the crowd.

Chapter ii

*W*hen Charlie made the dreadful call to tell Elizabeth he had been locked up, he lied about the circumstances of the arrest. He told his wife he was smoking weed on the steps of the brownstone they shared, and the police hauled him in. Elizabeth knew it was illegal for Charlie to have marijuana in his possession, but the amount of time Charlie was telling her he would get for illegal drugs didn't add up. Elizabeth didn't want her husband to get railroaded, so she did her research and secured a lawyer. She scraped up enough money for Lucas to start working on Charlie's defense. After Lucas took the case, he revealed why the state was asking for life: Charlie was being charged with first-degree murder. Once Elizabeth learned of the murder charges, she stopped paying the lawyer and she and Sam stopped visiting. Elizabeth refused to work two jobs to pay for a lawyer. She wasn't sure if Charlie killed someone or not, but the fact that he lied was proof enough that he wasn't where he was supposed to be. She had a son to raise and didn't want Charlie's evil spirit to influence Sam.

Charlie's trial lasted one week. He had no chance of surviving the jury trial, the semen analysis, the wallet in his duffle bag, and the fingerprints in the apartment sealed Charlie's fate. The jury convicted him within thirty minutes of deliberating of killing Janie Matthews, a murder he didn't commit.

Today Charlie sits in his cell wishing he never cheated on his wife. Over the years, he wanted to establish a relationship with Elizabeth and Sam, so he wrote Elizabeth letters, begging to see Sam, but to no avail. In her penmanship, she wrote with a bold marker "Return to Sender." Charlie's heart sank every time a letter was returned. He still keeps hope alive that one day he will see his Beth again, because one letter wasn't returned.

Charlie's attention is drawn back to his reality. His friend Charles is dead. Bruce opens the door to the cell with an empty box and haphazardly collects Charles' belongings on his side of the room.

Chapter 12

Samantha, startled at the sound of the ringing phone, jumps. Still lying on her back, she reaches for the phone with her left hand.

"Hello."

"May I speak with Samantha Walker?"

"This is she."

"Hi, my name is Janie Paisley. I am the desk clerk at Rikers Island, and I am sorry to inform you that your father, Charles Walker, died this morning. His wife, Beth Walker, couldn't be reached, and you are listed as an emergency contact."

"My mother is in an assisted living facility."

"We have your father's belongings and need to turn them over to the next of kin."

"I didn't know my father well. When I was a young girl, I remember going to visit him once in jail and my mother never took me back. I am not sure what possessions he leaves behind, but I don't want to have anything to do with him."

"Samantha, I've been on the job for twenty-five years and I've heard similar stories. Regardless of how you feel, you do have to collect his belongings and claim the body."

Samantha gazes at the ceiling.

"Samantha, are you still there?"

"Sorry, yes, I am."

"For what it is worth, I know you might not have known your father, but you can get some closure by doing the right thing; not only for your father but for yourself. You can go through what he leaves behind and understand who he is now. Your father was a model inmate. He worked in the kitchen and led Bible study for a small group of inmates. He was trying to make amends for what he did. Don't be so hard on him."

Samantha thinks about the conversation and her heart starts to soften. "I will be there today."

Chapter 13

Samantha drives the thirty-four minutes to Rikers Island Correctional Center, and the facility reminds her of her visit. Sitting in the car, she reflects on the last time she visited her father, Charles. An image that stood out the most was the separation between her and her father; she reached out to him but couldn't touch him or hold his hand. A glass separated her father from her mother. She could only hear bits and pieces of a one-sided conversation from her mother because she was speaking into the phone receiver. Samantha uses the palms of her hands to pound her forehead to remember, but the voices of the other visitors made it hard to hear the conversation between her father and mother. However, Samantha remembers the room; everyone was on the phone. Her mother put her hand to her mouth and cried. Through muffled sobbing she asked the love of her life, "Why, why did you do this? I love you. This will be the last time that you will see your family again." Abruptly, Beth hung up the phone.

"Get your coat, Samantha, we have to leave."

Samantha wailed, "No, I want to be with my daddy."

"Come here, little girl, we have to leave." Beth jerked Samantha's arm so hard it made a popping noise.

"No, Daddy, no. I don't want to go. I want my daddy."

Samantha pulls a napkin out of the armrest, wipes her face and eyes, blows her nose. She folds the napkin and blows again. She looks in the mirror and checks her nose to ensure nothing is left behind.

Samantha exits the car and walks to the front door of the Rikers Island administrative building, throwing the napkin in the trash. She squirts two medium pellets of antibacterial gel onto her hand and rubs them vigorously together. She waves her hands back and forth in the air to dry the extra gel that formed in between her fingers. While cleaning her hands, a gentleman walks up behind her and opens the door for her. "Thank you," responds Samantha.

"You're welcome," says the stranger.

Samantha looks the man over and notices he is wearing a name badge hanging on a lanyard around his neck. "Excuse me, Jerry. Someone called me earlier to pick up my father's belongings. He died earlier today."

"I am sorry to hear about your loss." Jerry extends his hand to Samantha and introduces himself.

"I'm Samantha Walker."

"Actually, someone from my office must have called you. Please, walk this way. I can help you get your father's personal effects."

Samantha follows Jerry to his office. He walks toward his desk and rolls his office chair away from the desk. Samantha has already found a chair in front of his desk and is seated. "What's your father's inmate number?"

"I have no idea. I barely knew him and never visited him as an adult."

Jerry knows this is common when fathers are incarnated when their children are young.

"Samantha, what's your father's name."

"Charles Walker."

Jerry shakes the mouse on his computer to take the monitor out of sleep mode. He types his password on the keyboard. He brings up the New York State Department of Corrections system and clicks on Rikers Island. Jerry's fingers dance on the keyboard. "Samantha, I found your father's information."

Jerry buzzes his secretary. "Linda, will you go into storage and retrieve the personal effects of Charles Walker. From looking at the items in the box, it should be light. If you need help, call me."

"I sure will, sir."

"Jerry, do you know the cause of my father's death?"

"Samantha, do you have any type of identification?"

"Oh, of course." Samantha searches her wallet for her driver's license. She fumbles with the hard plastic protecting her license, chipping her thumbnail. She finally retrieves her license and hands it over to Jerry. She chews on her nail to smooth the ridges.

There is a knock at the door. "Come in," says Jerry through a raised voice.

Linda appears with the box under her right arm. "Is there anything else, sir?"

"No. Thank you."

Linda walks out of the office and closes the door behind her. Jerry pulls out a form for Samantha to fill out to claim the contents of the box. He records her driver's license on both the form and into the computer. Jerry extends his arm over the desk and gives Samantha her license back.

"Thank you."

"We don't have the autopsy information. Once we get it, we will give you a call."

Samantha does not respond or react to the sound of Jerry's voice.

"Samantha, did you hear me?"

"Yes." She stares out the window. She begins to speak again in a shaky voice. "I didn't know my father well. He went to jail when I was a young girl. I visited him once and my mother never let me see him again. I didn't think much about him throughout the years until someone from your office called me to collect his belongings." Samantha frowns.

Jerry has lived a privileged life and can never think about not having a relationship with his father. "I tell you what, this is only a suggestion. Your father had a cellmate, Charlie; you should talk to him. He may be able to tell you something about your father to help you treasure his memory along with understanding the contents of the box." Before Jerry was a born-again Christian, he thought people got what they deserved, but his heart softened when he gave his life to Christ.

Samantha stands, slides her purse straps on her shoulder. "I'll think about it."

Jerry reaches to the corner of his desk and hands Samantha a business card. She slips the card in the side pocket on her purse. "I hope you can find closure."

"Thank you," says Samantha and picks up the box.

Jerry stares as the beautiful woman walks out the door.

Samantha places the box in the truck. She moves her hand gently over the top of the box. It's hard missing a man you never knew. Samantha closes the trunk of the car and fires up the engine to follow the sign to the inmate visitation room.

Chapter 14

Charlie is popular—two visitors in one day. Charlie thinks back over the course of his life, and he is not familiar with anyone by the name of Samantha. He shrugs his shoulders; maybe she is a lawyer in that bitch Marcia's law firm. *She thinks she knows me, but she does not. I have something for her.* His thoughts are interrupted when Samantha walks toward him. She sits quietly in front of him, and the clear panel separates the two of them. Charlie points to the phone over her right shoulder. Samantha's nervous stomach churns. The room starts to spin; she remembers the day her mother brought her here to visit her father. She vigorously wipes her sweaty hands on her jeans.

Charlie carefully observes his visitor. He's definitely never met her but notices she is extremely nervous. Samantha's chest rises as she inhales and blows air to relax. She sits back and picks up the phone slowly. "Hello." Samantha's voice is shaky, her mouth dry. She licks her lips.

Charlie not knowing what this meeting is about says nothing. He doesn't trust this Samantha person.

The air between them thick, the silence is deafening even though no one is speaking. Samantha clears her throat. "My name is Samantha Walker. My father was your cellmate."

Charlie uncrosses his arms and sits on the edge of his chair.

"Girl, let me look at you. Your father talked about you all the time. You have grown up to be a beautiful young woman."

Samantha blushes and smooths her hair behind her right ear.

"Charles said you were smart. What are you doing now? Doctor? Lawyer?"

"No, I recently left my position as a portfolio manager. I found some of the practices troubling…borderline unethical."

"Oh yeah! You just walked off the job and didn't have another job. That's interesting."

"I do pretty well for myself. I can afford to find my true purpose in life."

That sounds like white people bullshit, quitting a good job and trying to find myself. Charlie was at a loss for words.

Samantha shares her reason for the visit. "As you know my father died and I never had the opportunity to know him as an adult. Can you tell me a little about him?"

Charlie, who does not get many visitors, will give her just enough to keep her coming back. "Your father was a very complicated man." *Yeah,* Charlie thinks, being dishonest in his initial statement to Samantha. "Your father talked about the times the two of you would play hide and seek. One time the two of you were playing and you hid behind the drapes in the living room and your red sneakers were sticking out of the bottom. He said he spotted you instantly when he walked into the room but didn't want you to lose, so he sat on the sofa and waited before he tagged you. But he fell asleep." Both Samantha and Charlie laugh.

Samantha's bottom lip quivers as she remembers that day, because the next day her father was arrested for attempted murder. Samantha dabs the corner of her eyes and sits in silence while

Charlie tells her some wild stories—some sound familiar, others she doesn't remember at all. The story of her twelfth birthday party is odd. She never got a cat, her mother was allergic, and she never liked cats. And furthermore, her father was in prison by the time her birthday came around. Nonetheless, she listens to Charlie until visiting hours are over.

Samantha leaves the prison with more questions than answers of who her father really was. She rushes home to plunder through the contents of the box.

Chapter 15

Samantha balances the Chinese take-out while opening the door. The door slams with a push of her foot. She walks straight ahead and places her food on the kitchen island. She unfolds the top of the Chinese box and grabs a plate and scoops out a healthy portion of fried rice and then moves to the sesame chicken. She opens two packs of soy sauce with her teeth and pours the entire contents over her mound of food.

Samantha carries her plate into the living room, where she opens the lid of the box of her father's contents. Her eyes scan the box, trying to glean as much as she can about her father through a first glance of his property. She moves some things around and finds a picture. The woman has beautiful milk chocolate skin and silky, wavy hair. Samantha isn't sure who the lady in the picture is; she flips the photo over. The photo is tattered and the only words she can read are "to my darling Charlie." The photo is signed "xoxo." Samantha turns the photo over again; the lady in the photo doesn't look anything like her mother. The skin tone is much lighter. Her grandmother would call her high yellow.

Samantha lays all the contents of the box on her coffee table. One envelope with nothing inside, just an address on the front. Next, several letters written in a child's handwriting; a New King James Bible; a book called *Life Lessons* with a photo sticking out to either mark the page or to keep it safe; Charles' wallet; two stacks of letters, handwritten on the envelope in bold, "Return to Sender." Samantha's eyes move from stack to stack wondering where to start. She naturally is drawn to the handwritten letters in the script of a child. She slowly unfolds a letter one third at a time, and the blue ribbon adorns the words "first place," worn but still legible. *He did love me.* Warm tears flow down both sides of her cheeks; she reads the letter as she rubs the satin ribbon between her index and thumb.

> *Daddy,*
> *Mommy says I can't write you because I will be wasting my time because I won't see you for about 20 years. That's too long. I want you to remember me. I want you to remember me. Here is a picture of me and the trophy I won.* In the picture Samantha is holding her science fair trophy and wearing her red sneakers. Samantha cries she remembers being proud to win the science fair in which she beat Scott Pruitt, who won the previous year.
> *Luv,*
> *Sam*

> *Daddy,*
> *I don't understand why you aren't home when I come home from school. Mommy is sad all the time. She said you did something really, really bad and can't come home. She won't say what. Daddy, please come home. I won't go to school tomorrow and wait for you. Come home. I luv you, Sam.*

> *Daddy,*
> *You never came home. You don't luv me? I luv you. Why don't you come home? Auntie Emma says she can't go behind Mommy's back to*

*send letters anymore. This is my last letter. Come home. I printed our
address on the bottom of the letter. Come home.*

    Luv,

    Sam

Samantha uses the back of her hand to wipe the tears from her face. Her father did love her in spite of what her mother told her, and she now has proof. All those years in counseling for nothing.

Samantha, too tired to go through the remaining contents of the box, locks the door and gets ready for bed. She falls asleep with a smile on her face knowing her father loved her.

Chapter 18

After a long night and early morning with Nick, Marcia dashes home and showers and changes into a new power suit. Later that morning she sits at Rikers Island waiting for Charlie to enter. An electrifying tingle moves through her body as she thinks about Nick. She flips through Nick's notes of the unsolved murder he thinks is tied to Charlie.

"What is Miss High Society Lawyer doing here? To see me, her jail bird client." He points to himself.

Marcia smirks. "Why wouldn't I be here? I represent you."

"Most lawyers don't waste their time with face-to-face meetings. They normally send their paralegals to do the grunt work. But you...." Charlie shakes his finger at Marcia. "There's something going on because you've been here the last two days."

"I told the judge I would defend you and here I am."

"Are you in some kind of trouble with the judge? I wrote him for years and now you show up."

Marcia looks at her watch. She has paying clients waiting for her. She needs to move this along. "I know what you did."

"I've done a lot of things, so you have to be specific. I've lived what some may call a colorful life." Charlie cleans the dirt in his index fingernail with the fingernail of his thumb.

"There was a girl's body found in an alley with no identification, but she later was identified as Sheryl Davis. Your DNA was found on the girl's body; apparently you spit on her." Marcia shoves the crime scene photo in Charlie's face.

Charlie knows what happened when he killed the girl but did not know when or how she was found.

<hr/>

Henry, the manager of the kitchen, was pissed that Walter did not take the trash out from the bathrooms before he left the night before. Walter assured him all the trash was emptied. Henry props open the back door, which leads to the ally. Henry receives a text from his girlfriend as he walks to the dumpster and smiles. They make plans to have dinner at her place later. Henry, focused on responding to his girlfriend, stumbles and falls face first. "Ouch, damn it." Henry looks around to see what he fell over. He sees the lifeless body of the girl on the ground and crawls backward to the door. His back hits the door and he stops. He jumps up and opens the door and slams it behind him. He searches his pockets and realizes he lost his phone when he fell over the body. He uses the kitchen phone to call 911.

Once the call is placed, Henry opens the back door and looks around the alley for his phone. He takes pictures of the dead body and sends the image to his girlfriend. He paces back and forth until the police arrive. "Over here, Officer!" Henry is waving his hands in the air as though he is waving airplanes to land.

"Sir, did you discover the body?"

"Yes, I was taking the trash out because Walter lied to me last night and didn't take the trash out. Walter is a lying sack of…"

The two detectives, Nick and James, steal side stares, rolling their eyes at each other as Henry rambles about the trash when there is a dead body lying before him.

Nick, the lead detective, tries to guide the conversation back on track. "Sir, so you were taking out the trash."

"Right, I would not have been out here taking out the trash if Walter took the trash out last night."

"I understand the trash situation. Let's move past Walter not taking the trash. What's your name?"

What's wrong with this guy and the trash, James thinks. *If he's the manager, just take the trash.*

"So, what happened next?"

"I was taking the trash out and found the body."

"Did you see anyone in the alley?"

"No, I was texting my girlfriend and fell over the body."

Nick originally thought Henry could have been the killer, but he soon realizes throughout their conversation that he is too goofy to kill anyone.

While Nick is questioning Henry, Aaron, the patrol officer, has called the coroner. He took notes so when the detectives arrived, he could hand them over. Aaron looks the girl over several times and sees a discolored spot on her patent leather shoe. He picks up the shoe and places it in a plastic bag and labels it "right shoe." He does the same for the left shoe.

The officer's allergies are bothering him.

"Achoo!" He sneezes over the body. He rummages through his back pocket and wipes his nose with a handkerchief.

Nick looks over at the junior officer and can't believe what he is seeing. Did he just sneeze on the body? Nick turns his attention back to Henry. "Thank you for your help." Nick walks over to Aaron. "What are you doing?"

"What do you mean? I just bagged both shoes, and one shoe had something that looks like gum, maybe from the killer."

Nick gives Aaron an impatient look. "Where are your gloves? You have to use gloves."

———————————⊙———————————

Charlie grows impatient with Marcia. "No, I don't know what you are talking about. Do you have questions on my case?" He shoves the picture back in Marcia's direction.

"I don't have new developments as of yet."

"Guard!" shouts Charlie.

"I still have more questions on the murder of Sheryl Davis."

"I don't know any Sheryl Davis. Guard!"

Charlie leaves the room without answering Marcia's questions about the murder of Sheryl Davis.

Chapter 17

*S*amantha wakes bright and early to start her quest to find more about her father. She lingers over her father's belongings and chooses the empty envelope and the photo. She types the address in her GPS. She pulls in front of the home of Ms. Josephine Pearson—at least that's what's displayed on the front of the envelope. Samantha makes eye contact with the neighbor sitting on the porch to the left. Samantha nods and smiles. The neighbor abruptly leaves the porch. Samantha turns her attention to the task at hand: speaking to Ms. Josephine Pearson. Samantha marches up the walkway to the front porch. She takes a deep breath, rings the doorbell, and looks around the yard. She notices no car in the driveway. She rings the doorbell a second time, intrigued by the answers she will find about her father. Out of the corner of her eye, she sees the neighbor reappear on the porch. Samantha shields her eyes from the glare of the sun while eyeing the suspicious neighbor.

The neighbor uses the rails to balance her steps down the porch and walks to the street. The neighbor uses a notepad and pen to take down the make, model, and license tag number. Samantha then becomes equally intrigued by the neighbor. Her eyes follow the neighbor back to her front porch, where she sits and makes eye contact with Samantha.

Samantha turns away from the direction of the stranger long enough to push the doorbell again.

"She ain't home," announces the suspicious neighbor.

"When will she be back?" Samantha is unsure who "she" is but goes along with the conversation.

"Don't know."

"Can I ask you a question?"

"Depends."

After several minutes outside the door with no answer, she searches her purse for paper and pen. Samantha scribbles a brief message on the back of a receipt and places it in between the screen door.

Samantha turns and proceeds down the steps. She cuts across the heat-worn lawn to the neighbor's house.

"Hi, I'm Samantha." She extends her right hand.

"Nice to meet you."

The neighbor never shakes Samantha's hand; in the awkwardness, Samantha drops it by her side. Her smile wanes.

"My name is Mabel."

Samantha uses her eyes to make a snap decision about Mabel. She seems friendly enough. *Why didn't she shake my hand?* Perhaps she can trust her since she has no other choice. She begins to tell Mabel her story.

"A few days ago, my father died in prison, and the Bureau of Prisons gave me his belongings. He went to jail when I was twelve. I visited him once, but my mother was so angry with him for going to jail, she refused to visit. Of course, since I was a minor, I lost contact with him. I never got the chance to get to know him."

Mabel loves a good story, and this sounds juicy. "Child, come inside out of the heat. Let me get you some tea." Samantha follows Mabel inside the seventies-ordained house, with olive green carpet and furniture with olive green and orange flowers, and a sofa covered with a layer of thick plastic. Mabel motions for Samantha to sit on the sofa. The plastic squeaks under her weight as she sits. She moves again...*squeak*. Samantha's eyes adjust to the darkness of the room. Mabel reappears with a tray of two tall glasses of sweet tea with ice and two slices of pound cake. Mable places the tray on the coffee table. "Go ahead, help yourself." Mabel hands Samantha a napkin. Samantha takes a huge bite of the cake. The buttery flavored cake melts in Samantha's mouth. She chews the cake but could have let it dissolve in her mouth. She washes down the cake with a gulp of sweet tea.

"Child, would you like another piece?"

"Yes, please."

"Here, take my piece. I know better than to eat this cake with my sugar being as high as it has been these last couple of days."

Samantha gladly accepts the cake but takes her time and pinches off a small piece and places it in her mouth.

"Go on with your story of your father."

"Right. I was fine not knowing him, but since his death I've been obsessed about finding out who he is. I went to Rikers Island, picked up his belongings, and am trying to sort out what it all means."

"What did you find in the box?" Mabel takes a sip of tea.

"I found an envelope with the address of Ms. Josephine Pearson, which is why I was next door. There were letters from my mother, Beth, and other odds and ends." Samantha reaches in her purse. "I found this picture, but I don't recognize the person in the photo. It's not my mother."

Mabel is all into the story. She didn't know Samantha's father and asks to see the picture. "She is a beautiful young lady." Mabel hands the photo back to Samantha. "What's next?"

"I don't know. I visited his cellmate Charlie, and he was kind enough to meet with me. I learned my father tried to reach out throughout the years to contact my mother." Samantha grows quiet, then begins to verbalize her thoughts. "I wonder how my father knows Ms. Josephine? Can you tell me about her?"

"I don't know." Mabel doesn't want to relive the death of her friend Jossey. "Tell me about your father's cellmate?"

"Well, I don't know much other than his name, Charlie Evans." Samantha ponders the visit. "Actually, the entire time I was there, I only talked about my father."

"What did you say his name is?"

"Charlie Evans."

"I am not sure if your father knows Jossey, but Charlie lived with her and Michaela and perhaps she wrote Charlie and the envelope ended up in your father's belongings."

Samantha stares blankly at Mabel.

"I don't know the answers to who your father was, but I can give you a piece of advice about Charlie. Don't trust him because he is evil. I knew him when he was a child, and he is capable of killing. I know what I saw that day." Mabel takes a calculated sip of tea and holds the favor in her mouth before she swallows.

"What happened?" blurts an anxious Samantha.

"Charlie's parents hosted their annual Fourth of July cookout. You know I have a small bladder, so I had to make another trip to the bathroom. I turned the knob to the front door, and it was locked. You have all these people over and you lock the front door. I thought the whole situation was weird. She finally opens the door and tells me I can't use the bathroom downstairs and I have to use the one upstairs."

Samantha, on the edge of the chair, shouts, "Someone was dead in the downstairs bathroom."

"Do you know how the story ends or do you want me to finish?"

"Excuse me, please go ahead." Samantha takes a sip of her tea.

"I came down the stairs and heard a thump, so I went into the kitchen, and I was standing at the top of the stairs to the basement and there were two bodies wrapped in trash bags lying on the basement floor. When I went back outside, I did a head count. Dorothy and Daniel were missing." Mabel's voice trails.

Samantha, a quick learner, raises her hand.

"Child, just ask your question. You don't have to raise your hand."

"Who are Dorothy and Daniel?"

Mabel stands and tops off both tea glasses.

"Well, it was none of my business but Dorothy, Sharon's best friend, was having an affair with her husband Daniel. I saw how the two of them were looking at each other with those school-yard glances at the book club. I knew something was wrong when Dorothy started coming to the book club."

"Why?"

Mabel starts to chuckle. "She wasn't the reading type. She only came to get closer to Daniel."

"Oh."

"Anyway, back to the original story. I was taking my shower later that evening and noticed below my bedroom window Justin, Charlie, and Sharon carrying two bodies wrapped in trash bags placed in the back of Justin's truck. Before you ask, Justin was Dorothy's husband."

"Why would Justin help get rid of the bodies? Did he know one of the bodies belonged to his wife?"

"I told Sharon to tell him, so he knew."

"Ms. Mabel, that's a horrible story. Did you report the incident to the police?"

"No, we don't trouble the police when karma raises its ugly head."

"So, when someone goes missing, what do you tell people?

"He ran off with Dorothy, her best friend. Daniel always had a wandering eye."

Samantha changes the subject. "Why do you think Charlie had something to do with the murder?"

"Well, nothing at first but his behavior started to change after the death of his mother."

"I am lost. Did he kill his mother, too?"

"No, she stepped out in front of a city bus."

"Oh, Lord have mercy. Why would she do something like that?"

"I think it was guilt. She was holding a secret about her son killing her husband and friend Dorothy. You know your demons can cause you to do things you never dreamed."

"My head is spinning. I started out trying to find answers about my father, but now I think I need to speak for the deceased. I need to find answers and bring closure to the death of Dorothy and Daniel."

"If you are chasing the life of Charlie, you will go down a winding road full of death and destruction."

"Do you know the address of Charlie's childhood home?"

Mabel points next door.

"Where is Justin, Dorothy's husband?"

"He lives around the corner. Let me give you the address."

Mabel walks to her bedroom and finds her address book. She scribbles the address down on the back of a scrap piece of paper. "Here you go, sweetie." Mabel takes a seat. "What are you going to do next?"

"I don't know. Let me give you my phone number in case you remember something." Samantha tears a corner of the envelope and writes her number down. "Mabel, thank you for your time. You've been very helpful."

Mabel, liking her new friend, responds, "Let me know how this whole thing turns out with your father."

"I will. Thanks." Samantha is more confused now than when she started the day.

Samantha sits in her car, checks her watch, and pulls the picture out of her purse. *Who is the mystery woman in the picture?* She slips the picture back in her purse and heads toward the prison to pay Charlie a visit.

Chapter 18

*S*amantha waits at the visitors table for Charlie. She has so many questions to ask him. Charlie walks over to Samantha with a bounce in his step. He has a visitor— someone other than his attorney. "Hey, Samantha, it is so good to see you. I don't get many visitors and now two visits from you in a week. I feel honored."

An awkward silence settles between the two of them. Samantha stares at her shoes. "What's wrong?" asks Charlie.

"Oh, nothing." Samantha lets out a loud sigh.

"Hey, I am your friend. you can tell me." Charlie reaches across the table and takes her hand.

Samantha raises her eyes to meet Charlie's. "I want to know more about my father. When I was growing up mother cut my father out of all the photos and scolded me whenever I questioned her about him."

"Sure, where do you want me to start?"

"Just jump in. Is it okay if I record our conversation? I want to capture everything you say and replay it later."

"I don't see any harm in that." Charlie touches Samantha's

hand and draws it back quickly, not to alarm the guards. Two physical touches may get him thrown out of the visitor's room.

"Your mother, Beth, was a beautiful woman inside and out. Your father never forgave himself for the pain he caused her, which is why he pleaded guilty not to draw out a long trial. He was convicted of first-degree murder and sentenced to life in prison." The rest of the story is hard for Charlie to talk about, so he waits for Samantha to give him a signal she wants to hear more. Charlie looks around the room at the other inmates enjoying their visitors.

"Who did he kill?"

"Charles met his whore once a week at her apartment, where they enjoyed drugs and sex. Candy, his lover, complained that Charles was hoarding the drugs and not giving her enough to get her high. They argued, Charles and Candy tussled for the gun, and Charles shot Candy in the chest. He never denied that he shot her. From the beginning he felt sorry for what happened. Charles was determined to be eligible for parole in ten years for good behavior. He wanted to be there for you, for all your memorable firsts—baby, wedding, et cetera. He wanted to make up for all the wrong he caused. Your father loved you and only wanted the best."

Samantha starts to weep. Bruce notices Charlie's visitor is upset so he walks over and hands her a box of tissue.

Samantha dries her eyes; sits in silence. Charlie, not sure what to say, decides nothing is the best option since he rocked her world, telling her why her father went to jail. Samantha breaks the tension between the two of them when she reaches in her purse and pulls out a small, faded picture. "Can you tell me who this is? I found the picture in my father's belongings. It's not my mother or anyone I recognize."

Charlie places his reading glasses on his face to examine the photo closer. He flips the photo over. "This picture was in Charles's personal belongings? Bruce must have taken the picture by mistake. This is a picture of my wife, Elizabeth." Charlie smiles at the picture of his beautiful wife.

"Charlie, if this is a picture of your wife, then you should keep it."

Charlie shrugs his shoulders rears back in the metal chair. "She gave up on me and divorced me while I was in jail. What type of woman does that to her loving husband?"

Samantha silently stares at Charlie, not knowing what to say.

Charlie reaches across the table to give Samantha back the picture. "She sent me this picture when she still believed in me."

Samantha takes the picture and places it in the side pocket of her purse.

Charlie searches his mind. Are there other items of his missing from the cell? The return to sender letters he wrote Elizabeth were only for her eyes and not anyone else. He makes a mental note to search his cell for them. "You would tell me if you found anything I should know about."

Samantha bats her lashes. "Like what?"

Charlie senses Samantha is holding out on him. He squints. "What else did you find in the box?" He raises his voice one octave higher.

"I haven't gone through everything yet; at a glance, nothing seems unusual."

Samantha decides not to bring up the envelope with Ms. Josephine's address or the return to sender letters.

Charlie scratches his head before he speaks. "Hey, I have a favor to ask."

"You're not going to ask me to rob a bank or anything." Samantha laughs but stops within the sounds of the first "Ha." "I'm sorry. That was inappropriate and insensitive."

"No, that's nothing," says Charlie with a dismissive wave of his hand. "I got a new lawyer. Her name is Marcia Rhodes, and she has taken on my case."

"That's great." It never dawned on Samantha that Charlie could be innocent. Mabel's voice is in the back of her head.

"What I want to ask you. I was wondering if you didn't have any plans…"

"Charlie, it's okay. Just ask me."

"Will you sit behind me when my case goes to trial? My family and friends stopped visiting me a long time ago. My wife stopped bringing our son to visit, so I do not have a support system. I was framed for a murder I didn't commit." Charlie's eyes move to the floor, and he hangs his head.

"Hey, look at me. You took care of my father while he was incarcerated, so you are considered family to me. I will be honored to support you during your trial. I will be there every day."

Charlie smiles with pride at Samantha, as though she is the daughter he never had.

"I will come back some other time. I have to run some errands."

"Next week?" says Charlie eagerly.

"Yes, I will see you next week."

Charlie grins wide, exposing his gold tooth.

Chapter 19

*S*amantha exits the prison and walks toward her car thinking about what she will eat for dinner. The ringing of her phone distracts her from her food choice. The number unfamiliar. "Hello, this is Samantha." Samantha unlocks the car and takes a seat.

"Hi, this is Michaela; you left a note on my door wanting to speak with my mother."

"Thank you for giving me a call. I recently lost my father, who was in prison. We were estranged and I didn't know much about him. I found an envelope in his belongings with Ms. Josephine's address. I want to find out more about her and their relationship." If Samantha wants to search for truth, she needs to verify Mabel's version of the story. "Can I swing by this afternoon and speak with her?" Samantha bites her lower lip.

"Sure, you can come by."

"Thank you, I should be there in about an hour."

"I will see you then."

Chapter 20

Michaela dries her hands on the dish towel at the sound of the doorbell.

"Hi, I'm Samantha. Thank you for allowing me to come by to speak with your mother."

Michaela unlocks the screen door and steps aside.

Samantha walks into the house, and her mouth salivates at the smell of pasta sauce. Her stomach rumbles.

Michaela turns toward Samantha. "Samantha, I didn't want to tell you over the phone that my mother died years ago. I don't know how much help I can give you on the reason for the envelope, other than my mother writing to him while he was incarcerated. We were getting ready to eat dinner. You are more than welcome to join us."

Eagerly, Samantha responds, "Yes, I am starved."

Michaela yells upstairs, "Abigail, dinner is ready."

"Okay, Mommy," the young voice responds.

Michaela sets the table for three.

"Where can I go to wash up?"

"The bathroom is around the corner on the left."

"Thanks."

Samantha scans the pictures on the piano. One photo catches her eye. She picks it up and stares at the uncanny resemblance of a young Charlie. Samantha races back to the kitchen. "Michaela, who are the two people in the photo?"

"Oh, that's my mother and Charlie. His mother died and Mom took him in. She had a big heart."

Mabel's story is checking out.

Samantha reaches in her purse and pulls out the envelope with Ms. Josephine's address. "This is the envelope that was in my father's belongings. His name was Charles Walker. He had a cellmate named Charlie Evans."

"Now that name sounds familiar. Are you sure Charlie didn't kill your father?"

"You are kidding, right?"

"Not really." Michaela gives Samantha a weak smile.

Samantha remembers the photo in her purse. "Do you know who this is?"

Michaela takes the photo out of Samantha's hand, turns it over.

"No, but she looks familiar. It seems like I have met her before."

A plump, round young child enters the room and walks up to Samantha. "Hello, I'm Abigail. What's your name?"

"Hi, I'm Samantha, but you can call me Sam for short; all my friends do."

Michaela smiles at her daughter, who never meets a stranger.

"Did you wash your hands?"

"Noooo."

"Go wash your hands."

Abigail runs to the bathroom. The faucet turns on.

Michaela hands Samantha the photo of the unidentified woman. Abigail walks into the kitchen and sits. Michaela turns to continue to set the table. Samantha senses her cue to wash her hands for dinner and stop asking questions.

The three enjoy the spaghetti dinner. Samantha smiles at how smart Abigail is for a six-year-old. She can hold a conversation on any topic from her favorite book to science.

"The dinner was delicious." Samantha wipes her lips on the cloth napkin.

"Thank you."

Michaela stands to clear the dishes.

"Oh, let me help. You were so gracious to invite me for dinner; the least I can do is help with the dishes."

"May I be excused?"

"Yes, baby."

Abigail disappears up the stairs.

"What happened with Charlie's mother?"

"She committed suicide by walking in front of a bus. He didn't have any family; his father took off with another woman. My mother was lonely with me at boarding school in upstate New York, so she took him in."

"It seems like Charlie had a good foundation after his mother's death. How did he end up in jail?"

"When he turned seventeen, he moved out. It was for the best because my mom couldn't do anything with him. He started stealing from my mom. He then started stealing from the local convenience store. The owners knew what happened to his mother and wanted him to go to jail, so my mom would go around town paying for what he stole."

"That's horrible your mother had to endure such disrespect from Charlie."

"With everything he did to her, she still felt as though she let him down. When he went to jail for killing that woman, my mother was in bed for days. I suspect she probably tried to reach out to Charlie by writing to him in jail. Did you find any letters from her? I would be curious to know what she had written to him about."

"No. I haven't gone through the entire box. Did he ever marry? Kids?"

"Charlie was married once to Elizabeth; they had a son. The only reason I know her name is that Mother mentioned Elizabeth coming by after Charlie went to jail, asking for money to pay her rent."

Samantha reflects on the conversation she had with Charlie. "You know, earlier I had a conversation with Charlie, and he wanted to know if I found anything interesting in my father's belongings and for me to let him know."

"Hm, I'm not sure why your father's belongings would be of interest to Charlie but what I can tell you is he can't be trusted."

This is the second person who's told her Charlie isn't a nice man, and she needs to believe he can't be trusted. Samantha takes a deep breath. She thought Charlie was trying to help her understand her father, but maybe he is just playing her.

"I want to thank you for your hospitality."

"You are welcome. I know you want to get to know who your father was. But it seems you are finding out more about Charlie than your father. Let me know what you uncover."

"I will." Over her shoulder Samantha yells, "Goodbye, Abigail!"

Abigail runs out of her room to the top of the stairs and waves. "Bye, Sam."

Samantha turns, waves at her new friend. "Thanks again."

She heads home after a long day.

Chapter 21

*S*amantha kicks off her shoes at the door. She pours herself a glass of wine and walks into the living room to examine the contents of the box. She flips through the pages of a book, *Life Lessons.* A letter falls out.

> *Dear Charlie,*
> *I want you to know even though I couldn't save you I am helping your son Samuel and Elizabeth with a place to stay. Your childhood home I kept up the taxes and allowed them to stay. Your son is growing into a handsome young boy. I just want you to know I will look after them, but I can't visit you in that place. I tried to shield you from jail, but you kept making poor choices and I couldn't keep fighting for someone who thought the world owed him something. Your mother's death was tragic, but you could have had a good life. I hope you enjoy the book Life Lessons.*

Some of the lettering is faded, she imagines from tears either from Mrs. Josephine or Charlie. This is the letter that is missing from the envelope she has been chasing.

What to open next? Eagerly, Samantha moves to the stack of return to sender letters bound by the red ribbon with her name, Samantha. She remembers asking Ms. Ramsey, her English teacher, to help her print her name the length of the ribbon in a straight line. They tested on white typing paper until she got it down. Even with a careful tug the bow disintegrates in her fingers.

My Dearest Beth,

I am sorry for the mess I have caused for both you and Sam. I know what I did was wrong. I left you to fend for yourself while I'm in jail. I know I promised you a good life. I professed in front of God my love for you when I took your hand in marriage. This is why I want to confess to you the crime I committed. Please come see me. I want to be a man and look you in the eyes and tell you the wrong I did. Please come to see me and bring Sam. I miss you both.

-XOXO

Letter 1 Return to Sender Letters

To My Love!

I know it's been a few weeks since my last letter. I was thinking, if I'm going to be a better person, I need to be totally honest. You were right to not visit. I wasn't honest with you about the charges. I was unfaithful to you the day before I was arrested. I met Janie at the coffee shop. I was frustrated I lost my job. I'm not making excuses, but I didn't feel like a man. The weight of having a kid. Don't get me wrong, I love Sam, but it was too much. I needed something different. I wanted freedom, I wanted an escape, and Janie was it. I was going to run away with her. I didn't kill her. I promise. That's the truth. Come see me. I love you and Sam.

Letter 2 Return to Sender Letters

My Darling Beth,

It's been a month since my last letter asking you to visit me. I know I let you down, but I wanted to tell you what happened the day I was arrested. Since you never visited me, here's what happened. I know this is hard to hear, but I did plan to leave you and Sam. I'm not proud of my decision. I lost my job and felt horrible about not being able to take care of my son and went back to my old ways. I left the house every day to deceive you, plain and simple. One day, I left the house, met someone, and decided to run off with her the next day. If I had not cheated on you, I would be home with my family. When I walked into her apartment the day we planned to leave, she was dead. I stole her wallet but didn't kill her. I swear. I am now being what I should have been years ago, a man. Please, please come and see me. I want to know Sam. I love you!

Letter 2 Return to Sender Letters

My Love!

I want to find my way back to you, and in order for me to do that I need to be honest. The day you told me you were pregnant, I killed Sheryl Davis. That's why I had weed. Sitting here in jail, I know I had a good thing with you, and I foolishly threw it away. I have been living with this guilt for years. Will you visit? I want and deserve to see Sam.

Chapter 22

Samantha pours herself a bowl of cereal and sits on the sofa. Her eyes move from her father's belongings and rest back on the book called *Life Lessons*. She reads the author biography and the inside flap. She turns the book upside down, the spine of the book gaps between the hardback and the cover. She closes one eye to look down the spine, where something is wedged in between. She uses the tips of her fingers to try to pull out the piece of paper. Samantha races into the bathroom and finds tweezers to pull the letter from the spine. The letter is folded many times over, small enough to fit along the spine.

You thought you could have sex with my wife, Janie, a married woman without consequences. All afternoon I waited across the street waiting for you to leave to end my suffering. I killed her so you would know how much I was hurting inside. You are in jail facing life in prison. I hope you are thinking long and hard about what you did to me. If I couldn't have her, you wouldn't either, so I killed her. I sliced her with a knife and waited in the apartment until morning and slipped out the back. I waited until you were inside to call the police. Sitting across the street, I had a perfect view of you being arrested in the backseat of the police car.

Samantha gasps. She searches her mind to the day she saw Charlie's lawyer on television. She calls Marcia Rhodes' law firm.

"May I speak with Marcia?"

"May I ask whose calling?"

"Samantha Walker. I am a friend of Charlie Evans…"

"She's not available."

"I have evidence that Charlie Evans did not kill Janie Matthews."

"Please hold." Connie immediately calls Marcia. "I have a Samantha Walker on the line; she says she has evidence Charlie Evans didn't kill Janie Matthews."

"Connect us, I want to talk to her."

"Samantha Walker, I have Marcia Rhodes on the line."

"Hello."

"Samantha, this is Marcia Rhodes. How can I help you?"

"My father recently died, and he was the cellmate of Charlie Evans. In my father's belongings I found a letter from the killer, Edwin Matthews, Janie's husband. In the letter he admits he killed his wife."

"Can we meet so I can see the letter?"

Marcia and Samantha decide to meet.

Marcia, still at the jail, requests the visitors log and asks about the death of Charles Walker. Samantha's story checks out. Marcia calls her investigator to find Edwin.

Chapter 23

Karen, Marcia's investigator, goes to the house of Janie's husband, Edwin. Camila opens the door. "How can I help you?"

"I'm looking for Edwin."

"He's not home." She pulls down her sleeve to cover her bruised arm. "What is this about?"

"A man is serving life in prison because it is alleged, he killed Janie; there is a confession letter where Edwin says he couldn't imagine his wife being with someone else and killed Janie. I need help proving this man's innocence. Is there something you can tell me to help him?"

Camila twirls her hair. "You need to go. My husband may be watching the house. I mean coming home soon."

"Okay, are you available to meet me for coffee tomorrow? There's a coffee shop in the strip mall. Let's meet tomorrow at 7:00 in the morning. Does that work for you? An innocent man is getting a second chance for his freedom at the Appellate Court. I need you to give a written statement or testify to clear his name."

"We'll see."

Camila closes the door as her husband drives up in the driveway.

The investigator, not wanting to bring additional doubt toward Camila, waits on the porch for Edwin to approach her. Camila listens intently on the other side of the door. "Hey, sorry to bother you—have you seen my dog? A Yorkshire terrier, Jewel. She ran straight out the garage as I was letting it down. Have you seen her?"

"No, when did she run away?"

"Last night. I've been looking for her all night and day."

"Sorry, but we haven't seen any lost dog."

"Thank you for your time." Karen walks slowly to her car and waits for Edwin to close the door before speeding down the street.

Chapter 24

*K*aren, the investigator, arrives at the coffee shop a little before 7:00 a.m. to meet with Camila. Fifteen minutes after the hour, Karen gives up on Camila and orders a large coffee and a breakfast sandwich. She takes a seat at the back of the coffee shop, her back to the door. Around eight o'clock, Karen walks to her car wondering why Camila didn't meet her for breakfast.

"Hey!" The investigator turns around, and in the car next to hers is Camila. A baseball cap pulled tightly on her head, sunglasses shielding the shiner to her left eye.

"Camila, is that you? I didn't think you would show. Can we talk?"

"Get in."

The investigator opens the passenger door and faces Camila.

"Are you okay? Your lip is bleeding."

Camila reaches in the armrest for a napkin. She dabs her lip while wincing in pain.

"I'm having a hard time trying to get the answers I need for the murder of Janie. But the elephant in the room is the abuse."

Long silence between the two of them.

"Is your husband doing this to you?"

In a soft whisper she responds, "Yes, but it doesn't happen often."

"The fact that it's happening at all is a problem."

"You don't understand."

"Try me, make me understand."

Camila changes the subject to what Karen wants to discuss. "In Edwin's abusive rants, he told me if I ever went to the police, I would end up like Janie."

"End up like Janie? Did he mean dead, or he killed Janie and you will end up dead? Sorry, I'm confused." A man's life is on the line, and she needs Camila to be specific.

"He told me he killed Janie and I would end up dead just like her."

"We are going to trial tomorrow, and you have the abusive statements of your husband that he killed Janie. You have to say something. You have to go to the police."

"He would kill me if I told the police. Where would I go? I don't work or have money. He controls the finances. There aren't any assets in my name."

"I'll talk to Marcia to get you protection, and I can help you find a job. Will you consider going to the police?"

Camila takes a deep breath. "I'll think about it."

"That's all I can ask. How can I get in contact with you? I don't want you to get in trouble with your husband." Camila shakes her head.

"Don't judge me!"

"I'm not. You feel you are in a tough situation, but a man will go to prison for the rest of his life. He doesn't have a choice, but you do. You stay with a man who's abusing you."

"I don't know. I can't make any guarantees."

Karen opens the door.

Camila yells, "You can't come back to the house. Edwin might get suspicious."

The investigator slams the door without looking back. She gets in her car and speeds away.

Chapter 25

*S*amantha arrives at the court by 8:30 a.m. Enough time to grab a coffee at the local coffee shop. Samantha marches up the steps of the courthouse and finds the trial room for Charlie. She sits in the front row so Charlie can feel her presence.

Judge McCaskill enters the room. Marcia and others in the room stand.

Marcia rolls her eyes at the sight of Judge McCaskill. He smiles in her direction. "You may be seated."

Charlie glances over his left shoulder—no Samantha. He sighs, and his shoulders slump. He turns his head to the right, and Samantha smiles. Charlie grins, his gold tooth shining in the light. He sits back in his chair; confident he has someone to support him.

Marcia takes the stand to make her case to acquit her client. Marcia opens with her client entering the house of his lover and being at the wrong place at the wrong time. Her abusive husband entered the apartment prior to Charlie's arrival. Samantha listens to the events of the case, which sound similar to the letter she read in her father's belongings.

Marcia tells the court they have a witness, Edwin's current wife, who has signed a statement that Edwin confessed he killed his first wife.

Bruce shackles Charlie slowly. It gives him a chance to talk to Samantha. "Thank you for coming. This means the world to me."

"You were my father's friend; this was the least I could do for you."

Marcia places the strap of her purse on her shoulder, briefcase in hand. She exits the courtroom in a huff. Samantha rushes the conversation with Charlie. "I'll see you soon."

"Marcia, what's next?"

"We wait to hear if he is found innocent or guilty. Thank you for what you found. It can help him."

In a low whisper, "Charlie may not be guilty of this crime, but I'm not sure about the death of his father, Daniel, and his mother's best friend, Dorothy."

"What information do you have?" Marcia is intrigued. She knew Charlie was guilty of something.

Samantha goes through what she found in her father's belongings and how it ties to what she uncovered in her amateur investigation. "Keep me posted on what you find out."

"Will do."

Chapter 26

Samantha takes the journey to Justin's house, seeking answers in his wife's death. A lady wearing scrubs answered the door, with a name tag of "Precious." She opens the door with a warm smile.

"Hi, my name is Samantha. I'm looking for Justin. I'm assisting Marcia Rhodes, an attorney, in the disappearance of Dorothy. Is Justin available to talk?"

"He's available to talk but you may not get much of an answer out of him. He has early stages of dementia. That's why I'm here to help him around the house, a few days a week. Come in." Precious opens the screen door. "He's out back in the sunroom watching westerns. If you need anything just holla."

"Justin, my name is Samantha Walker. I'm helping Marcia Rhodes, an attorney, find answers in the death of your wife, Dorothy."

"I was never married to anyone by the name of Dorothy. Margaret died last year. She really loved me, and I loved her."

"I'm sorry to hear about Margaret."

A tear rolls down his cheek. "Samantha, have you ever been in love?"

Samantha ponders the question. "Yes, once."

"You know how your heart flutters when they call. You miss them as soon as you close the front door. My Dorothy knew she had my heart."

Samantha squints while Justin tells her the story of the love of his life. "Is it Dorothy or Margaret?"

Justin smiles as he remembers the last time, he saw her. "The Fourth of July was hotter than any other Fourth of July. The weatherman said it was over 100 degrees with the heat index of 105, but my Dorothy still wanted to go to the annual cookout her friend Sharon hosted. Dorothy got up real early to fix a pasta salad."

Samantha pulls out pen and paper and starts to take notes. "We had a good time with friends; the majority of the people at the party were neighbors. Mabel, Josephine, Ella...it was a bunch of us." Justin's smile wanes. "Sharon was a good friend to me and Dorothy. Dorothy and Sharon go way back to high school. I met her when Dorothy and I started dating. It just wasn't right." Justin shakes his head and turns his attention back to his westerns.

"What wasn't right?"

"I'm getting tired. Margaret, I'm ready for my nap."

Precious helps Justin to his feet. He drags his right leg as Precious guides him to the bedroom, takes his shoes off, and pulls the blanket across his body.

"See you when you get up, Justin."

"Thanks, Margaret."

Samantha walks toward the front door. "Precious, who is Margaret."

"Margaret was his second wife."

"And Dorothy was his first?"

"Yeah, he loved Margaret, but Dorothy was his world. Her cheating on him with her best friend's husband was devastating. He didn't date for years until he met Margaret at church."

"He said she died last year."

"That's correct, she died from kidney disease. She was caring for Justin before she died."

"Has Justin ever talked to you about what happened to Dorothy?" Samantha asks in a whisper.

Precious motions with her head to move the conversation to a more private area just in case Justin isn't asleep. "I can get fired if he found out I told you. In all his rants, I was able to piece together that Sharon caught Dorothy and her husband, Daniel, having sex on the Fourth of July celebration. An altercation occurred where the son Charlie stabbed Dorothy and killed her."

"Where's the body?"

"If you noticed Justin has a limp. The last construction job he was on before he went out on disability, he hurt his leg. There was a big ordeal about who was to blame. The construction company abandoned the project and is suing the city, so the project stalled."

"Where is the site and what were they planning to build?"

"Apartments on the corner of Stonewall and Caldwell. Well, they were going to build apartments on the lot."

"Do you know who owns the property?"

"Wilson & Wilson owns the property. Theodore Wilson checks in on Mr. Justin every now and then. He evens pays for his doctor's visits. Theodore pays me directly. I can't complain. My check is direct deposited every two weeks."

"That's odd, if the construction project wasn't complete, why is Theodore still paying Justin?"

"Justin was the foreman and a dedicated employee. Every now and then Mr. Justin has the phone on speaker, and I can hear every word of the conversation, not that I want to. Listening to the conversation, it seems there's more to the story than I know. Theodore seems to be keeping the lot out of obligation."

"What do you mean?"

"Yeah, Justin wants to stick it to Theodore, but it seems there is guilt. I can hear it in his voice."

"Maybe Theodore feels guilty because Justin got hurt at work?"

"Maybe. Theodore is still mad at the city and won't sell even though they haven't finished the building and it is an eyesore."

"Thank you for your help."

"Have a nice day."

Samantha walks to her car with a grin on her face; she is driving to the site of the apartment building. Samantha drives by the building and finds a parking spot. She finds it hard to view with the underbrush and weeds. Samantha scribbles down the name and number on the construction sign and places a call. "Hello, may I speak with Theodore Wilson."

"He's unavailable. May I take a message?"

"Yes, tell him Samantha Walker. I am working with Marcia Rhodes, attorney at law." She gives the secretary her name, reason for calling, and phone number. Samantha drives home.

Chapter 27

While driving back home Samantha gets a call from Theodore Wilson. "Hello."

"Hi, this is Teddy Wilson; I had a message to give you a call."

Samantha pulls over on the side of the highway to safely speak with Teddy and take notes. "I am working with attorney Marcia Rhodes; she is defending Charlie Evans. I wanted to ask you about the disappearance of Dorothy Baker."

"Very tragic."

What's tragic? Quickly she makes Teddy an offer. She needs to see his facial expressions when she asks the question. "Teddy, can we meet this evening for an early dinner and drinks?"

Samantha picks a restaurant two doors down from the deserted lot he and the city are fighting over.

Samantha picks up the phone and makes a call. "Marcia, we have a problem. Remember when I told you I was going through my father's belongings."

"Right, what else did you find." Marcia was rushing Samantha along because she heard that part of the story.

Samantha ignores Marcia and continues the conversation at her own pace. "It looks like Charlie's possessions were mixed up with my father's stuff. Charlie killed his father. Meet me at 8:00 this evening." Samantha gives her the same address she gave Teddy earlier.

The hostess sits Samantha, who orders a glass of white wine. The hostess escorts Teddy to her table. Samantha stands and extends her hand to Teddy.

"Samantha, nice to meet you."

"You as well. Thank you for agreeing to meet. I know it's last minute."

When the waitress brings Samantha's drink, Teddy is eager to place his Macallan order.

Samantha knows this is going to be an expensive conversation, so she dives straight in. "On the phone earlier, you mentioned Dorothy's situation was tragic. What did you mean?"

"Her death…it was tragic."

"How do you know she's dead? All I hear is she is missing." Samantha takes a sip of wine.

"Well, after all these years, she's probably dead. You know what they say, if someone isn't found within twenty-four to forty-eight hours, they are dead."

Teddy takes a sip of his drink.

"I think police say that about children when they go missing." She looks directly into his eyes.

Teddy picks up the menu and covers his face.

The waitress reappears. "Have you made up your mind about dinner."

"I'll have a salad with chicken."

Teddy, on the other hand, says, "I'll have a Porterhouse steak cooked medium well. You can throw in a salad for color." Teddy's smile is crooked and his cheeks red. "Will you bring me another?" He shakes his glass at the waitress. Samantha looks at the almost empty glass. He puts the glass to his mouth and drains the expensive drink.

"Teddy, how well did you know Justin on a personal level? I know he worked for you before the accident."

"He was my foreman; he and I are old friends. We played golf on the weekends."

"So, you knew his wife Dorothy too?"

"Yeah, she would come over to the house from time to time. I mean I knew her."

"What type of relationship did you have with Dorothy?"

Teddy sips his fresh drink.

"Listen, Dorothy was friends with a lot of people. If you know what I mean. I would wine and dine her and buy her gifts her husband couldn't afford." The Macallan is making it easy for the truth to come out. He takes another swig of his drink. "Right before Dorothy went missing, she told me she was pregnant, and the baby was mine. How would that have looked if she had my baby and is married? Justin and I were friends."

Now he has a conscience. Samantha tries really hard not to judge.

"I told her she needed to have an abortion and that was that." Teddy takes another sip of his drink. "She told me she wanted to leave her husband for me." Teddy leans into the conversation. "I wasn't going to leave my wife for someone everyone in town had a piece of."

"I see" is Samantha's only response. She takes a sip of wine.

"She told her husband that I was the father of the baby. So, when Justin called me that night and asked to use the apartment site to dump the body, I agreed. I have my morals; I asked if he killed her. He promised me he didn't do it. After betraying him, I felt like I needed to help. Do something because of the pain I caused him."

"Let me get something clear, you thought it was helpful to him to cover up a murder."

"You are twisting my words. Justin told me this kid Charlie accidently killed Dorothy. I believed him. Justin is a solid person, not his wife." Teddy's eyes are wide. He takes a deep breath. The burden has been lifted after all these years.

"Is this why after the lawsuit you didn't do anything with the building?"

"I was between a rock and a hard place. If the crew started working on the building, someone may find the body. If I sold the property, someone would find the body." Teddy holds up his hands, which are balled in fists. "I stood solid as a rock." Teddy takes a sip of his drink.

"Do you want to do the right thing and go to the police?"

"Hell no! I'll go to jail. I'm not stupid."

Samantha finishes her salad and wine in silence. What is she going to do about it? "Would you sell the building to me?"

Teddy has suffered losses during the economic downturn and wouldn't have been able to afford the meal, especially the Macallan. "Let me talk to my realtor and get back to you."

"Okay, sure."

The waitress stops by the table to collect the empty plates. "Did you make room for dessert?"

Samantha jumps in so Teddy doesn't order anything else. "We are good. Just bring me the check. Thanks."

"I want to thank you for a lovely evening."

"Thanks, Teddy. We will be in touch."

As Teddy leaves the restaurant, Marcia enters.

Marcia scans the restaurant and finds Samantha. "Wow, you really hit me with a bombshell this evening."

Samantha signs the credit card receipt. The waitress places the card holder in her apron.

Marcia directs her statement to the waitress. "Will you bring me a martini?"

"Absolutely."

"So, tell me what you found in your crusade to find out who your father was. Did you get the answers you needed?"

"I got sucked into following the contents of the box but found out more about Charlie than my father."

"How does something like that happen?"

"My father's name was Charles, who has a daughter, me, Samantha. My friends and father call me Sam for short. Charlie has a son named Samuel and goes by Sam as a nickname. All the letters that I was tracking down were addressed to Beth. My mom is Elizabeth and Charlie's wife's name is Beth. I thought I made a connection with my father reading one of the letters, thinking he loved me, but it was Charlie professing his love to his son Sam."

"Where is the missing letter? Who has it?"

"Finish your drink and we will go and get it."

Marcia throws back her martini and the two leave the restaurant.

Marcia and Samantha arrive in a middle-class neighborhood. They both exit the car and knock on the door.

The door opens. "Hello?"

"Hi, my name is Samantha Walker, and this is Marcia Rhodes, attorney for Charlie Evans."

"Let me guess. He wants my address to send me more of those letters."

"Not exactly. I met Charlie when my father died, Charles Walker, his cellmate. I found the return to sender letters that were mixed up in my father's belongings."

Beth slams the door in their faces.

Samantha and Marcia are expressionless. "Why did she slam the door on us?"

Beth swings the door open and hands Samantha the last letter, unopened. "I want this nightmare to be over. Don't ever come by here again. I don't want anything to do with Charlie, ever." Beth slams the door again. This time Samantha and Marcia leave and go home.

Chapter 28

Marcia and Samantha sit in the car waiting for Charlie's release. Marcia was notified two hours in advance that Charlie would be released, and she reached out to Samantha. Charlie, a free man, walks toward the gate with his belongings in a bag over his shoulder. Marcia, an excellent attorney, smiles; she got Charlie off for the killing of Janie Matthews, a woman he never killed. Just in the wrong place at the wrong time. This seems to be the theme of his life.

Samantha and Marcia were busy the last week. Teddy sold Samantha the vacant lot on the corner of Caldwell and Stonewall and excavated the entire lot to find the bodies of both Dorothy and Daniel. With the bodies and the letters, Marcia convinced a judge of Charlie's guilt.

The gate opens and a police car pulls up in front of Charlie. Two officers exit the car. "Charlie Evans, you are under the arrest for the murder of your father Daniel Evans and Dorothy Baker." The officer places handcuffs on Charlie and shoves him in the backseat of the car.

Samantha breathes a sigh of relief. Marcia turns to her. "I couldn't have done this without you. It sounds like you may have found your new career."

Samantha smiles. "Maybe."

www.ingramcontent.com/pod-product-compliance
Lightning Source LLC
Chambersburg PA
CBHW030528260626
47157CB00005B/1930